FALLING THROUGH
THE WORLD

Rachel ××

First published in Great Britain in 2012
by Lunette Publishing

Copyright © 2012 Rachel Clarke

The author asserts her moral right to be identified as the author of this
work under the Copyright, Designs and Patents Act 1988

This novel is a work of fiction and, except in the case of historical fact,
any resemblance to actual persons, living or dead, is purely
coincidental.

A CIP catalogue record for this book is available from the British
Library.

ISBN: 978-0-9573370-0-8

Cover Design by
Chandler Book Design
www.chandlerbookdesign.co.uk

Printed in Great Britain by
MPG Biddles Ltd

FALLING THROUGH THE WORLD

Rachel Clarke

LUNETTE PUBLISHING

Prologue

Ali dropped the card off on the way to her last exam. I could hear her talking to Mum in the hallway. The subdued murmur of their voices reached me like a faint echo of another life. After a while, I heard the gentle click of the front door – doors didn't slam in this house anymore – and I knew she'd gone. I imagined her striding off down the drive, back into that other reality where I could no longer follow her.

Later, Mum brought the card up. She smiled down at me in bed before taking it carefully out of its envelope, making sure the paper didn't rattle too much. Then she propped it on my bedside table and sat wordlessly in the chair beside me, staring silently into the darkness. We stayed like that for an hour or more until it was time for her to go back down and make lunch.

When she'd gone, I reached out for the card. My arm burned with the effort of lifting it; my head felt muzzy. I strained to focus. A chubby bear stood clutching a huge silver key with the number 16 emblazoned across it. Its glowing face and rosy cheeks positively radiated health and well-being. Inside was one of those printed verses about being "Sweet Sixteen" and all your dreams coming true. Ali had drawn an arrow coming from it with the word YUCK!!! written in bold capitals, followed by several exclamation marks.

I smiled, remembering the day Ali and I had run round the card shop in town competing with each other to find the cheesiest verse until the shop assistant'd had enough and kicked us out. I screwed up my eyes, trying to block the rush of misery and longing that surged through me.

That was the *real* Sarah, the real me. *'Not this, not this!'* I repeated over and over, the hiss of my voice fading against my cracked lips. Perhaps, if I closed my eyes for long enough, this wouldn't be happening to me: if you don't walk on the cracks, then the bears can't get you. I held my breath for a full minute until I could see stars beneath my closed lids. Then I opened my eyes, ready for a miracle but the world was just the same: the blacked-out window panes, the tomb-like silence of my room and my burning, aching body: the wretched shell of a human being.

I didn't want to stay there. Instead I decided to join her, that other Sarah – the real me. I knew the only place I could reach her now was in memories so I closed my eyes and slid gratefully into the past. The birthday card fell from my hands and I was fourteen again, sitting with Ali on the plastic moulded chairs of the Community Centre, at one of those hideous family dos, you know, the sort where you take one look around and just pray you were adopted! Not my family this time; it was Ali's sister's sixteenth and I'd been invited to keep Ali out of trouble. **BIG MISTAKE!** We'd located the drinks' table in about five seconds flat and had already siphoned off half a bottle of vodka into our long glasses of lemonade. Suddenly, everything became ridiculously funny, even the pervy jokes Ali's uncle kept making about everything being legal when you turn sixteen.

'Hope that includes putting members of your family down,' Ali cringed as her father gyrated across the dance floor in a way that must have been deeply embarrassing to anyone who knew him, even twenty years ago.

I spluttered, rather too loudly, into my lemonade causing a collection of nearby aunts to tut disapprovingly. And that was when we decided. We'd gang up when it came to our sixteenth and insist on a party for us and our mates, strictly no family allowed!

The noise of a car horn outside dragged me cruelly back to the present. There'd be no party for me now, only another day of the same stubbornly familiar four walls with their insistently cheerful lemon hue and that crack in the ceiling which seemed to be gradually evolving into a deep immovable gash. How could I have slipped so far from myself, from the girl who laughed a little too loudly at a party to the one who lay here, day after day, trapped in this dark tunnel, this shadow of a life?

I knew there must have been a moment when I could have stopped it, when I could have held on tight to the world, stood firm and simply refused to let it all happen. Day after day, I traced and re-traced my life, desperately trying to find the moment where it had all gone wrong, to stop time and put it right again.

But where to start? I cast my mind back for the millionth time and arrived at that Friday, a warm day in early spring only a little over a year ago. I was rushing excitedly through the empty school corridors desperate to let Ali in on my big news and stubbornly ignoring what my body was already trying to tell me . . .

THE FALL

Chapter One

By the time I reached the girls' locker area it was deserted apart from two Year 8s, in a corner, squealing over some glossy magazine and Ali, of course, who stood leaning against our row of lockers sighing and looking theatrically pained. She was making small stabbing gestures at her mobile and from the look on her face, I rather suspected she was pretending it was some sort of voodoo doll made in my image. When she caught sight of me, she waved it frantically in the air.

'Where on earth have you been? I must've sent about a dozen texts!'

'Sorry,' I gasped, scrambling through my bag to find my mobile. 'I've not switched it back on yet.'

Ali rolled her eyes and I sank down onto the floor to reach my locker. You see, in our school, you either have a top locker which means you get to practise beheading people when you open it or, like me, a bottom one so you end up crawling round on your hands and knees and generally showing your knickers to the world every time you want to get a book out.

'So?' Ali demanded.

'I had art,' I said as though that was some sort of explanation in itself which, to be fair, if you knew our teacher, it probably was. Ali looked unimpressed though. 'Well, you know what Thompson's like.' I buried my face defensively in my locker and started to dig out my PE kit. 'She's had us standing there all afternoon, sun right in our eyes, trying to catch the essence of a table leg or something like that. You know what it's like: half an hour of that new age dribble and you sort of stop listening. Anyway, I'm completely blinded by the sun and I go and spill half a ton of paint all over the floor literally two minutes before the bell and, of course, she makes me clear it all up which took about half an hour but then . . . guess what?'

'Well, I'm guessing it's not that you came rushing here to meet your long suffering friend.'

'Not ex-actly,' I squirmed, feeling slightly guilty. 'I was on my way here, honest, but then I ran into Dan and . . .' I paused for dramatic effect, jerking my head up so I could see Ali's reaction. She was busy deleting messages from her mobile. '. . . he asked me out to the cinema tomorrow night!'

'And the surprise is?' Ali's eyes didn't even flicker from her touch screen. 'About time as far as I'm concerned! I mean, you two have been simpering round each other for weeks. I was torn between getting a sick bucket and locking you both in the storeroom till you'd actually managed—' she suddenly broke off and looked straight down at me. 'Hey, what'ya wearing?'

I froze in panic. 'I hadn't got that far!'

'You can borrow my new top, if you want.'

'What, really? No way!'

That's just like Ali. I mean she calls a spade a spade, as Grandad used to say, but she's dead nice underneath. Plus, she just happens to be in possession of the most gorgeous, expensive top I've ever seen. It's got this amazing neckline: not really, really low so you're hanging out all over the place but just right, you know, sort of sexy but subtle at the same time. You see, we're the same size, me and Ali, which is pretty much it as far as looking alike goes. I'm blonde and well, let's face it, a little on the short side whereas Ali's five foot nine at least with dark skin and jet black hair which makes her pretty distinctive looking, particularly round here which isn't exactly the multi-racial capital of the universe!

We're talking suburbiaville: think immaculate lawns and identikit houses, parents whose dreams revolve around their kitchen extensions and kids who just want to get as far away as they can before they turn into replicas of them. Mind you, it's too late for some. Take Chloë, this girl in our class. She's spent the last two months boring everyone stupid, going on about the huge en suite bedroom she's going to have when her parents move to this swish new executive home. In form period this morning she excelled herself: fifteen solid minutes of every tedious detail you could imagine. Ali was sitting beside me, scribbling away, desperately trying to finish her history homework. All the same, I could feel the pressure building and finally, sure enough, she cracked.

'Great,' she announced, cutting short a particularly lengthy description of matching floor and wall tiles, 'you can go to the toilet in your bedroom! Can we change the subject now? This isn't exactly helping me write about the Industrial Revolution, you know.'

'It's not my fault you've left your homework till the last minute, again,' Chloë sniffed. And with that she stuck her annoyingly pretty little nose in the air and made it clear she wasn't talking to either of us. No great loss, of course, but all the same, I'm not quite sure how *I* got blamed for it. I did snigger rather loudly but I suspect it's more to do with the fact that Chloë's got this major crush on Dan and seems to think I'm some sort of evil femme fatale, luring him away from his true destiny.

Dan. The thought of him suddenly made me panic. I mean, I liked him. More than that, he was gorgeous. Half the girls in our year had a crush on him but hours on end alone together? What if we had nothing to say to each other? What if it turned into a repeat of the Mark Lewis fiasco?

Mark Lewis – that was a thought I did *not* need to have right now! What can I say? It seemed like a good idea at the time. He was this boy in our class, not exactly ugly, no major mental incapacity and he could string a sentence together. Not really a glowing recommendation but you haven't seen the rest of them! So, anyway, when he asked me out, I was like, yeah, all right, that'd be great. You see, the problem was, I'd never actually been out with anyone before and I was just so relieved someone had finally asked me that I jumped at the chance without really thinking if I liked him or not but there was nothing there between us, you know, no spark and the date was like this major disaster: we just sat there stiffly in the cinema, staring rigidly forward, extra careful not to brush against each other for two excruciating hours. I think we were both relieved when it was all over. And then, two weeks later, Mark's dad got this job in America and the whole family moved away. I don't think there was any connection to our date but Ali remains to be convinced. Oh well, as long as Dan didn't leave the country, I suppose it could only get better.

'*He-llo!* Earth to Sarah!' Ali was frowning down at me. 'Are we going home or are you planning to spend the night in your locker?'

'Sorry.' I dragged myself back and grabbing my last few books, got to my feet. As I stood up, I felt weirdly dizzy. The world seemed to whizz past me and I had to grab hold of Ali to steady myself.

'You OK, Sarah?'

'Yeah, I-I'm fine. I've just been feeling a bit gooey all day, you know, like I'm coming down with flu or something. Could really do without it, to be honest. I mean, I'd better not have a cold or something for tomorrow night.'

Ali hoisted me up. 'Oh, you'll be fine. Just dose yourself up on aspirin. My sister did half her exams like that and she was all right. Anyway, there's no way you're backing out now. Nothing's going to cheat me of the look on Chloë's face Monday morning when she finds out.'

'Don't worry. I'll be on that date even if it kills me! Purely for your sake, of course.'

'Come on, then,' Ali laughed. 'We'll go round to mine and check out that top.' And picking up my PE kit, she started to haul me towards the door.

Chapter Two

I was as good as my word. The next evening saw me leaving the cinema with Dan. We were laughing about the dire film I'd managed to pick. We'd just spent the last ninety minutes watching some gormless bloke's attempts to get various women into bed being continually scuppered by his little brother, all in the name of his loyal ex girlfriend. Throw in some predictable "hilarious consequences" and a sickly sweet Hollywood ending and really it was enough to make you vomit! To be fair, though, pretty much anything could have made me vomit by then. The flu had come on with a vengeance and, despite the industrial strength painkillers I'd found at the back of our bathroom cabinet, I was feeling pretty queasy. I was determined not to let anything get in the way of enjoying myself with Dan, though, not after the endless weeks I'd spent wondering if he actually liked me.

As we stepped outside, he turned to me. The corner of his lip tilted in a half smile; a flop of fair hair fell over his dark eyes. I felt my stomach lurch in a way I knew had nothing to do with the flu.

'So,' he asked, 'is it really that bad having a little brother?'

'Worse!' I pulled my face into an exaggerated grimace. 'But Jack's not that little anymore. He'll be thirteen next week and believe me, there's nothing cute about him. Mind you, you don't actually see him these days. You just sort of hear him stomping about in his room with his music playing *really* loud.'

'Oh and I suppose you keep yours down at a nice sensible volume,' Dan joked, that half grin still teased across his face.

'Naw, but my music's not rubbish, is it?'

'Of course not!' Dan was laughing out loud now; I grinned stupidly back. He flipped his wrist round and glanced down at his watch. 'D'you fancy, I dunno, going to the park or somewhere to sit down for a while? We've got plenty of time.'

It was still only half past seven. We'd had to go to the early showing at the cinema because my parents always insisted I was back home by nine. It was seriously embarrassing but it did mean, as Dan said, that we now had plenty of time.

I hesitated for a moment. It was starting to get dark. I looked out past the car park to the uninviting black mass beyond it. Then I turned back to Dan. He had a mole on his cheek, about an inch from the corner of his mouth, and when he smiled in the full, open way he was now, it disappeared into a sort of dimple.

'OK,' I agreed.

He led me across the floodlit car park, taking my hand easily, naturally. Our linked fingers slid against each other with every movement. My heart beat high up in my throat; I couldn't speak.

He helped me over the crash barrier but I stumbled anyway, lurching clumsily into him. He caught me and brushed the hair back from my face. My forehead felt hot under his cool, dry fingers but I had no idea if that was because of his touch or just one more symptom of the flu. I could hear his breathing inches from my ear. It fanned out across my cheek in hot, short bursts. I stood waiting, barely daring to move. His lips parted in a smile. I thought he was going to kiss me but then quite suddenly, he dropped my hand and ran off towards the children's playground.

'Come on!' he yelled over his shoulder.

I followed more slowly. The ground was grassy now, heath-like and uneven. My stomach lurched violently with every step; something sharp stabbed behind my eyes: the painkillers were wearing off.

Ahead of me, Dan leapt over a seesaw. He skimmed its surface with ease. Then, panting slightly, he perched himself on a low wall beside a distinctly muddy looking sand pit. I finally caught up and settled myself next to him, straddling the wall so that we sat facing each other. It felt good to be sitting still again.

I looked up and caught his eye. My body felt like an awkward mass of arms and legs. I racked my brains for something clever or funny to say but came up against a brick wall of agitated dullness.

'So you haven't got any brothers and sisters, then?' I finally managed, moaning inwardly at the sound of my own voice. I mean, how pathetic can you get? It sounded more like I was opening a letter to a pen pal than trying to embark on a passionate affair. Dan didn't seem to notice, though.

'No, it's just me and Mum at home. Pretty quiet most of the time apart from when Dad comes to see me.'

'Your parents are divorced?'

'Yep. It's been ten years now. You know, I reckon most parents sort of chill out after a while. They either get all civilised and become friends or they just stop talking altogether. Not my parents . . .' he paused for an instant, looking back towards the neon lighting of the multiplex before going on in a half mutter. 'Still, it *is* my fault they split up in the first place so I can't really complain.'

I didn't think that could be true. Dan caught the look on my face and waved his hands out before him, laughing slightly, 'Yeah, yeah, I know, like major cliché – kid of divorced parents thinks it's his fault they split up but in my case, it's sort of true.'

'Yeah?'

'Yeah, you see, when I was a kid I didn't much like wearing my seatbelt and Dad was never that good at checking on stuff like that. Anyway, this one time, when I was five, Dad was taking me swimming and I deliberately didn't do my belt up. I'd just seen this really amazing film on TV. I can't even remember what it was called now. I mean, it was probably rubbish but you know what it's like when you're a kid and you get totally caught up in something. Well, it had this car chase in and I was dying to swing round the back seat like they'd done in the film. Only, there must have been some fault with the door or it wasn't closed right in the first place because I slammed into it as the car took the first big corner and it swung right open and I just sort of rolled out onto the road.'

'No way! Were you badly hurt?'

He didn't answer me directly. Instead, he leant his head forward and brushed aside the thick hair that grew down the back of his neck. Underneath, the skin was damaged: shiny and bumpy looking, not the striking scarlet of raw pain but the faded dullness of old scarring. It felt like he was showing me something private, intimate almost.

'I was off school for months after that, first in hospital, then at home on the sofa, listening to Mum and Dad tearing strips off each other. You see, Mum blamed Dad for the accident. She's never really forgiven him. I don't know what was up with Dad. Maybe he felt guilty or maybe he was just fed up with being yelled at all the time but he was so angry – having a go at Mum and me, kicking the furniture, breaking plates and stuff. Actually, they both did a fair bit of that but it'd never be their fault, you know. They'd always blame the other one. Every day I'd think it couldn't get any worse; but it did. Then three weeks after I'd gone back to school, Dad just disappeared off to Manchester. That's where his parents are from, you see. He phoned me a few days later, told me how everything'd be so much better that way. All the usual rubbish, you know. I didn't really see much of him for years after that. I think he avoided coming down because every time he did, Mum and him started screaming at each other again . . . and that's the way it's been ever since.' He stopped short. It was like he'd suddenly snapped shut. He stared past me, back towards the cinema. His face was set, like he was sitting on an overloaded suitcase, determined to keep the lid down.

'Yeah, but it doesn't make it your fault they split up, does it? I mean, it probably wasn't even the accident. People don't just get divorced over one thing, do they? There was probably loads of stuff, long before that you just didn't notice.'

His eyes slid over me. 'Yeah, maybe,' he shrugged. 'It just seemed like one day everything was OK, then I go and catapult myself out of the car and suddenly the world's turned upside down. D'you think things can happen like that, that quickly, I mean?'

'I don't know, I don't think they do with divorce, not usually, anyway but with other stuff, I-I'm not sure . . .' I thought about Grandad and the morning Mum's sister had phoned to say he was dead and it'd felt like a hole had been punched out of the world where bloody-minded, lovely old Grandad had stood just the day before. 'Yes,' I said, staring vaguely at the sandpit. 'Yes, I think things can happen like that . . . sometimes.'

I turned back to Dan. I wanted to tell him about Grandad but he wasn't looking at me anymore. He was staring fixedly down at the wall, tracing the mortar of the brickwork with his forefinger. The sleeve of his sweatshirt had ridden up and I could just make out the fine golden hairs scattered over the olive skin of his forearm. I watched, silently, as his finger covered the distance between us. He reached my knee and stopped abruptly. We looked up at the same time.

I felt the breath shuddering in and out of my body. There was an intense, almost questioning look in Dan's eyes as he lent forward to kiss me. The world around us seemed to shrink. For a moment, I froze completely, surprised by the new sensation, the moist tingling pressure against my lips. I'd never kissed anyone before, not properly anyway, just quick jokey pecks under the mistletoe at Christmas, nothing like this. After a second, though, I found myself returning the pressure and putting my arms round his neck. My fingers found the scarred area beneath his hair. I stroked it lightly. It stretched over the undamaged skin around it and felt smooth and tight. I pressed hard against Dan's lips, trying to block out the pain. He tasted of popcorn and mints – sharp and sweet; my body arched closer to him; our legs wrapped round each other, the tough fabric of our jeans rubbing together. Dan's hand strayed under my top. I didn't stop him. I didn't know when I would stop him. I mean, I wasn't going to have sex with him, not by some dodgy sandpit on our first date but at the same time, I didn't think I ever wanted this to stop.

I spun on a roller coaster of sheer sensation. One minute, I was buoyed up by pure adrenaline, by the million tiny sparks that shot through my body as Dan's fingers ran up my back, the next I found myself plunged back down by the pain in my head and the fluey haze that was gathering ever closer around me.

I clung tightly to Dan as he traced the edges of my bra. Then, all at once, I just knew I was going to be sick. I pushed him sharply away, struggling to disentangle my legs.

'What? What is it, Sarah?'

But I couldn't answer. I just held my hand up to quieten him. Finally I got my legs free and half slid, half toppled off the wall. I bent double on the ground and found my face inches from the sandpit.

I put a hand to my mouth and clenched my stomach tightly closed. Whatever happened, I'd hold it in. I might be inexperienced but I was fairly sure that throwing up on someone you'd just snogged was a pretty major breach of dating etiquette! The wave of nausea passed but I got the feeling it'd be back soon.

'You OK, Sarah?' Dan had climbed down from the wall and was bending over me, his face drained of colour.

'I-I don't feel well,' I stammered. 'I have to get to the toilet.'

'Er, right, OK, then.' He looked nervously around. 'W-we'd better go. There's some back at the cinema.'

I wanted Dan to hold my hand, to tell me everything'd be OK. I was so scared. I didn't want to be alone with the frightening sickness, the plunging dizziness and the terrible pains that were wrenching through my body but, if anything, he seemed determined *not* to touch me. He kept a safe distance between us as we walked back to the cinema, giving me nervous, sidelong glances, like I was a bomb that could go off at any minute. Mind you, he wasn't that far off the mark. Let's just say I reached the toilets not a moment too soon. I left Dan, without a word, flung the door open and dived into one of the empty cubicles.

When I finally emerged, rather unsteadily, some fifteen minutes later, I walked straight into Dan who'd planted himself right outside the door of the Ladies.

'Look, I'm sorry,' he blurted out. 'I thought you were OK. I-I didn't mean to do anything to upset you.'

'What?'

'Well, we were like, you know, and then you suddenly run off like that and well, I . . .'

I wanted the ground to open up and swallow me whole. I mean, could things actually get any worse? Not only had I narrowly avoided vomiting over my first ever snog, the very guy I'd been dreaming about for months, but now he thought I was some sort of vestal virgin, running off to hide in the girls' loos if he even so much as touched me.

I took a deep breath and, summoning all the conviction a person can who's just spent the last fifteen minutes with their head down a toilet, I looked Dan straight in the eye and said, 'I *am* OK with it! I just don't feel very well, honestly. That's why I went to the toilet. I think I'm coming down with flu or something.'

'Oh, that's all right, then,' he said brightening. Me feeling ill was obviously the best news he'd had all week! 'I'll take you home.'

'No!' I cried a tad more fiercely than I intended. A woman coming out of the toilet stared at us curiously; Dan looked embarrassed. 'I mean, just walk me to the bus stop: I'll be fine.'

The fact was I'd told my parents I was with Ali. It wasn't that they'd mind me going out with someone. I'd just wanted to avoid all those tedious explanations and I really hadn't felt strong enough for the "being responsible" lecture, not today. Plus, if I'd told them, they might have wanted to meet him and that would've been too embarrassing for words. It'd just seemed easier to tell a few little white lies but how could I explain all this to Dan with my head spinning and the sickness rising up in me again? The room lurched as a wave of people surged past us. I gripped the wall to steady myself and quite suddenly felt too ill to care. I'd sort it all out with him tomorrow when the world was back up the right way again.

'Let's just go,' I begged.

So we walked to the bus stop in silence. The bus was just setting off when we arrived. I summoned my last bit of strength and sprang onto it. I didn't want any long goodbyes. The last thing I needed was Dan trying to kiss me goodnight with the taste of sick still on my lips!

I paid and collapsed into one of the front seats. I think it was supposed to be reserved for the elderly or disabled but I didn't care. Cold sweat ran across my forehead; I gripped the arm rest for support. As the bus drew away, I raised a hand to Dan but he didn't see me. He stood, hands in pockets, looking vaguely about him, an expression of hurt bewilderment spreading across his face.

Chapter Three

I never thought I'd be glad to see the inside of a maths room again but it's amazing what five weeks of flu does for your boredom threshold. *Five weeks!* And just my luck that two of them were the Easter holidays when I might have been doing something a tad more entertaining than lying in bed, feeling my head pound in time to Jack's abysmal music!

It had just gone on and on, day after groggy day of staring up at the cracks in the ceiling. Mum'd ended up having to take time off work to look after me. She'd used up all her leave and after that she'd gone half demented, dashing to and fro between work and home, checking I was OK. She'd started to look pretty haggard herself!

Plus, it took Dan a good two weeks of me missing school to work out it wasn't just some elaborate plot to avoid him. After that, though, he started sending me loads of really cute texts. He hadn't actually come round to see me but there again, I hadn't exactly encouraged him to. Let's just say I wasn't really looking my best.

But then, finally, at the beginning of last week, my head had started to clear and I'd just decided, *that* was it – I *had* to get out of my bedroom.

So, here I was, Monday morning, sitting in my first lesson – maths! I looked over at the clock – 9:48 – still three hours to go before I was due to meet Dan at lunchtime. Ali sat beside me, staring fixedly at the board with that look of aggressive determination she reserved only for maths lessons. Miss Freeman stood at the front, ranting away about algebra. I followed Ali's gaze and tried to concentrate but the figures on the board looked blurry. Maybe I needed glasses. I blinked and re-focused: $2 \ldots x \ldots$ the square root $\ldots$

Now, I'm usually pretty good at maths. It's like the numbers arrange themselves into patterns in front of me and I can just sort of feel my way to the right answer but I couldn't make sense of any of it today. I rubbed my head violently with my fists, trying to clear a pathway for the figures to get through and glared back at the board as ferociously as Ali but it was no good. I told myself I'd obviously missed something vital while I'd been away but I couldn't help thinking it was more than that.

Things hadn't been right all day – not since I'd left the house anyway. Somehow I was out of step with the world: the birds cheeped with an insistent screech, the sun shone too brightly and Ali seemed to talk non-stop all the way to school. I couldn't take it all in.

Now, sitting in class, I could hear every shuffle, every squeak of the board pen and the shriek of Freeman's voice. It felt like someone had fed every little sound into loudspeakers and shoved them right up against my ears.

I tried to pay attention but there was too much going on. My head began to throb. I decided the best thing I could do was just try and keep going till lunchtime. Seeing Dan'd put me right.

Eventually, the bell wailed: break-time at last! All I wanted was to get out of that stuffy room and sit down somewhere quiet with my chocolate bar – try and get the energy up for my next lesson but Freeman was making a beeline for me. She looked dangerously purposeful.

'Feeling better?'

'Mmm, thanks,' I muttered noncommittally. I shoved my pencil case down into my bag. Maybe if I didn't look up at her, she'd go away. No such luck.

'Right, well,' she continued, 'we've covered a lot of new ground while you've been away. Not to worry, though. A bit of extra work on your part and you'll catch up in no time. I can run through the most important points—'

'What? Now?'

She raised her eyebrows. 'Well, unless you think there's something more important you should be doing?'

I sank back down into my chair, defeated. There was no point arguing, not unless I wanted the usual lecture on how this was for my benefit, not hers and how if it was up to her, she could think of a million better ways to spend her break-time etc, etc, etc. I just knew I didn't have the energy for all that, not today!

Ali squeezed past me. 'I'll wait for you outside, OK?' She nodded towards the corridor. 'Have fun!'

Freeman pulled up a chair beside me and tucked her short brown hair behind her ears in a way that clearly meant business. I watched her pale hands with their long thin fingers as she outlined equation after equation on the pad of paper between us. I tried to follow her explanation but her words floated around me like fragile bubbles, too flimsy to grasp.

Outside, in the corridor, Ali scuffed her shoe noisily against the floor; the echo of it scraped through my ears. The too strong sun poured in through the oversized windows, pounding like lead against my throbbing temples and my head, my head was like cotton wool, so thick and fluffy that nothing could get through. Xs and ys circled my brain. I concentrated harder, straining to focus on the figures before me. Pins and needles shot through my left eye and circled outwards across my face. I started to panic. What was happening to me?

The room was suddenly silent. The incomprehensible flow of Freeman's explanation had stopped and she was looking at me expectantly. My heart sank: she'd obviously asked a question.

I stared down at the page. The numbers that usually flowed so easily, stood before me, bold, confident and completely meaningless, like the symbols of some unknown language whose dictionary I'd mislaid. I stared back at Freeman, vacant panic written across my face.

'Come on, Sarah. What's up with you today?'

The silence in the room grew; I shifted slightly in my seat; it was starting to get embarrassing; I didn't know what to do. Freeman frowned across at me. After what seemed like an eternity, she put us both out of our misery by answering her own question, 'You have to find the square root on both sides. Right?'

'Yeah, I see,' I lied enthusiastically, my one thought to get this interminable maths lesson over with. I wasn't fooling anyone, though. Freeman sighed and snapped the pad of paper closed.

'We're not getting anywhere, here, are we? Look, I've got a cup of coffee waiting for me in the staff room. Why don't we go on with this in a few days when you've got back into the swing of things?'

'Th-thanks,' I muttered vaguely. I had to get outside and escape the muzzy haze that seemed to have settled over the room. Somewhere, far away, Ali pushed the door open and stared at me, a funny expression on her face. A thousand pin pricks of light filled the room. I turned to Ali to tell her that people really did see stars before their eyes. It wasn't just something that happened in cartoons but the words never came because at that moment the world was ripped from me. Light and air, speech and breath, vanished in an instant as I was plunged deep into a vat of viscose liquid.

A wave of nausea ran up from my belly hitting my chest with a searing pain. My body burned red hot. I was overwhelmed by pain and panic as I struggled to find air but someone was forcing my head down deep into the thick unbreathable blackness. I had no idea what was happening. I thought I was going to die but just as the pain became unbearable, I seemed to rise up through it and back out into the light and air. I could hear Freeman's voice, calm and clear.

'It's all right, Sarah: you fainted. You'll be OK in a minute.'

The world returned to me slowly: the coarse utility carpet of the maths room, a jumbled view of my thighs, the hem of my skirt and Freeman's hand on my neck, pushing my head down between my knees with textbook precision. I took a deep breath. I longed to be able to speak again if only to tell everyone that, whatever the textbooks say, forcing someone's head into their bum isn't the most relaxing way to bring them round from a faint!

After a few minutes, Freeman began to release her iron-clad grip on my neck. I sat up slowly, tentatively. I leant my head back against the nearest table leg and opened my eyes. The sun streamed in making a curious patchwork of light and shadows amongst the cluttered mess of table and chair legs. Freeman and Ali crouched on either side of me, Ali's face tight with anxiety. I felt my breathing slowly return to normal. I savoured the air as it flowed smoothly in and out of my lungs. The terrible pain in my chest and overwhelming sickness seemed to lessen with each fresh breath. I felt relief flood through me at my sudden release from that terrible world of wrenching pain but it was short-lived. My breathing may have eased and the hot flush cooled but I still felt shaky and weak. The sickness, the dizziness, the headache were all still there in the background, prowling my body like a stalking animal, ready to pounce at my slightest movement.

'Are you OK now, Sarah?' Freeman asked.

'Y-yes, I think so,' I stammered but more because it seemed like the right thing to say than because it was actually true.

Freeman seemed to understand, though. 'You'll feel better in a minute,' she assured me. Then, after a slight pause, she asked, 'Did you have any breakfast this morning?'

'W-What?' I was confused. What exactly did a bowl of cornflakes have to do with finding myself sprawled on the maths room floor? 'Well, I—'

Ali cut sharply across me. 'Yeah, she did! She had two pieces of toast,' she lied. I'd actually had a bowl of cereal and that was ages before she'd turned up. 'I saw her eat them *and* she didn't go to the toilet to puke them up again afterwards. So she's not bulimic either!'

'Thank you, Alison! I think that makes things perfectly clear.'

Anorexia! Freeman thought I'd fainted because I hadn't had any breakfast. If only it was that simple. I had to smile, though, as the rather unattractive view I'd just had of my thighs would have assured anyone that I certainly wasn't starving myself!

'Right,' Freeman continued, business-like as always, 'you just sit there quietly for a few minutes while I get my things together. Then we'll take you along to Sick Bay.'

I nodded but my heart sank. Sick Bay meant Matron phoning Mum. It meant Mum taking even more time off work and her colleagues backbiting about having to cover for her, yet again. It meant Dad muttering about how we were going to pay the mortgage if Mum lost her job and, all round the house, it meant the tight strain of nobody knowing how to put things right.

Misery settled over me. Through the open window, I could hear the rest of the school at break: the chatter, the shouts, the screams of 900 people running round on a hot spring day. I wondered what it might be like to be any one of them. Whatever their problems, suddenly nothing seemed as bad as being trapped in this room, in this body that could plunge me, without warning, into such pain. Anything, I thought, just for this not to be happening to me.

'You OK, Sarah?' Ali asked.

I was beginning to wish people would stop asking me that. I mean, the answer was fairly obvious, wasn't it? But it was like they thought if they just kept saying it often enough, it would somehow *make* everything OK. I knew Ali was only trying to help, though, so I smiled and gave the expected 'yes'. Then I closed my eyes again so I wouldn't have to see the frightened, uncertain look on her face.

Chapter Four

Ali popped the chocolate into her mouth and began to chew vigorously.

'You pig!' I cried. 'That was the last caramel.'

'Stop moaning and eat the fudge. You're an invalid; it'll be better for you – less chewing!'

Her voice was thick and sticky with chocolate. I glared at her, trying not to smile as I shoved *both* the remaining fudges into my mouth. As usual, I wasn't really mad at Ali. After all, she was the one who'd actually bought the chocolates and made the whole class sign the card she'd got for me. I imagined her standing threateningly over everyone until they'd come up with a suitable message.

Mind you, some people obviously hadn't needed any encouragement. Chloë had taken up a good half of the card with her large round handwriting. I'd nearly vomited when I saw the sickly little hearts she'd used to dot her "i"s. She'd written some insincere gush about how much she missed me. Yeah, right, I thought. More like she can't wait to get in there with Dan. In fact, she was probably sticking pins in some voodoo doll of me right now. It certainly felt like someone was! Two more weeks had passed since that day in the maths room and I was still stuck in bed with the longest running flu in history.

I leant back against the headboard and scanned the messages. Most of them were pretty uninspired – lots of *Best Wishes* and *Get Well Soon* and loads of people who'd just signed their names. I searched for Johnny and Steve's messages. They're like the jokers of the class and let's face it, I could do with a laugh.

Steve had written some elaborate message in red ink, which he claimed was blood, pleading with me to come back soon and save them all from Ali. He said she'd beaten him up three times in the past week and was giving him the evil eye even as he wrote and Johnny—

I snapped the card shut and reached out an arm to catch Ali who was spinning wildly round on my desk chair, chewing on her next chocolate. The chair jerked to a halt. I felt the vibration of it judder up my arm and through my body. I closed my eyes for an instant to fight off the sudden wave of sickness.

'What?' Ali cried, swallowing the rest of the chocolate in alarm.

I took a deep breath and opened my eyes to fix her with a level stare. 'Ali, why *exactly* has Johnny written *Congratulations, you're expecting!*?'

'Ah, that,' Ali mumbled sheepishly. 'That was Chloë. You know what she's like. Well, she's been gossiping about you for ages: like one minute making out you're pregnant and the next that you're anorexic, you know, just because you passed out and feel sick and stuff. Well, I tried to ignore her, like pretend I was way above it all but then the other day in history she was in overdrive, saying all this stuff about you in her usual stage whisper and I just sort of lost it. So I turned to her and said, "Yeah, that's right. She's a pregnant anorexic smack head. You've got it in one!"'

I sunk my head into my hands and wondered, not for the first time, if having Ali as a best mate was really such a good idea.

'Thanks for throwing in the drug habit.'

'Yeah, yeah,' she went on, waving my thanks aside, 'but the really funny thing is, I swear, just for a split second, she didn't *get* I was joking. Her mouth sort of dropped open and she looked so excited, like she'd picked up some really juicy bit of gossip and then Johnny and Steve just cracked up and it's like a big joke—'

The crumpled heap on the bed that was me let out a stifled moan.

'On *her*, I mean, not on *you*. No-one really thinks you're pregnant. I mean, if Johnny even thought there was a chance you might be, he'd never write it in the card. He'd be too freaked out. You gotta see—' she broke off abruptly. I looked up to see what was wrong but she was staring fixedly down at my bedspread. She seemed to be finding its rather dull pattern a little too fascinating for my liking.

'Sarah?' she asked, keeping her eyes fixed downwards. 'There's no chance . . . I mean, y-you're *not* pregnant, are you?'

'No! *I told you.* All we did was kiss and I felt ill *before* I went out with Dan, didn't I? I wish I *was* pregnant. At least then I'd know there'd be an end to it!'

Ali looked up. Relief flooded her face. 'Anyway, that doctor of yours said it was glandular fever, didn't she? I'll tell them that at school. It should stop them. I mean, even Chloë can't make anything out of that, can she?'

'Well, the doctor didn't exactly say it *was* glandular fever. Just that it sounded like a classic case of it. I've got to wait till the blood tests come back to find out for sure. You wouldn't believe how much blood they took, tubes and tubes of it and not just those little test tubes but big fat boiling tubes. I'm sure they're not allowed to take that much even when you're like fit and donating the stuff. I mean, if you're not feeling ill before hand—' I stopped short, clapping a hand to my mouth.

'What is it now?'

'What if I've given it to Dan – the glandular fever, I mean? It'll be so embarrassing. Everyone'll know we've been kissing.'

Ali raised her eyes to heaven. 'I think we all just about worked that one out for ourselves. Anyway, has he actually been round to see you yet?'

It was my turn to stare down at the bedspread. 'N-no. It's hard for him,' I mumbled defensively. 'I mean, for a start, I'd have to tell my parents about him and besides, he's not very good with illness, you know, after what happened when he was a kid – all that time in hospital and his parents splitting up and stuff.'

Ali looked distinctly unsympathetic. To be honest I was getting pretty sick of it myself but I couldn't bear anyone else criticising him. They didn't know him like I did, didn't understand what he'd been through.

'Anyway, he did send me Dermot, here.' I nodded towards the seriously cute teddy with its red and blue knitted jumper that had arrived by Special Delivery a few days before.

Ali studied the bear with evident dislike.

The bear stared contentedly back at her, a fixed smile on its face.

I said nothing.

Chapter Five

Dr Passford was making frantic pecking movements over the computer keyboard and frowning up at the screen. She seemed only vaguely aware of our presence. Mum and I exchanged glances. I slumped a little lower in my seat. Forty-five minutes on the hard plastic chairs of the noisy waiting room had brought me close to death. The pains in my neck were so bad I could barely sit up.

Mum cast yet another anxious glance in my direction.

'You OK?' she mouthed.

I was so sick of that question! I mean, what *exactly* did she plan on doing about it if I turned round and said, 'Well, no actually, I'm not!'

'Fine,' I hissed.

Mum rolled her eyes towards the ceiling which irritated me even more. Static bounced in the air between us. Turning back to face Dr Passford, we both stared expectantly at the computer, waiting for my test results, hoping that somehow the answer would pop out at us but all we could see were scrambled words and frozen icons.

Dr Passford sighed.

'I'm sorry, the new system's supposed to make things easier but as usual, it's not working.'

I got the feeling this was her constant lament and we were supposed to cluck sympathetically at the trials of her life but, to be honest, I was all out of sympathy. My main focus was on staying alive long enough to find out what was wrong with me! Mum made the right noises but I could see her heart wasn't in it. Her face was tight with anxiety.

We waited patiently as Dr Passford hit the keys with increasing desperation and finally delivered a sturdy kick to the tower drive in an attempt to restart it.

'Ahh, we have lift-off!'

I sat boggled by page after page of my medical notes. Rows and columns of meaningless figures flashed before us. Dr Passford examined each one closely, nodding and frowning in turn in a way that made me wonder how long I had left to live. After what seemed like an age, she looked up at us and beamed.

'Good news! The test results are clear. There's no sign of any thyroid or adrenal abnormalities, diabetes or glandular fever.'

I blinked. *Not* glandular fever? Don't get me wrong. It wasn't like having it was a particular ambition of mine. It was just that when Dr Passford had said about it before, everything had made sense. I mean, people my age got glandular fever, they were ill for a while and then they got better and everyone understood what was going on. But now . . .

Mum seemed stunned too. I could see both relief and anxiety flicker across her face but mainly, she just looked confused.

'Well, what is wrong with her, then?'

It was the doctor's turn to look surprised. Her smile froze and frown lines appeared across her brow. She obviously hadn't been expecting that question. I found myself stifling a giggle although deep down, I was very far from finding any of this funny. I'd thought being a doctor meant you understood when people were ill, you found out what was wrong with them and did something about it, not that you plodded your way through a standard set of questions, sent for routine tests and then if someone didn't fit any of the boxes, threw your hands in the air and said . . . and said . . . what?

We were still waiting for Dr Passford to stop frowning and actually say something . . . anything . . .

I felt a tremor run through my world. The level surface of the ground split and a pit of loneliness and fear opened up beneath me. I found myself slipping into it. Had my body managed to invent a completely new illness? Would I have to go on feeling ill for the rest of my life because nobody knew what was wrong with me?

Panic crept up on me from every corner of the room, from the neat rows of medical textbooks, to the window with its narrow view of the brick-walled alleyway, to the door through which I longed to escape, healthy and whole again.

The pain was nearly unbearable now. I felt sick beyond words. The room began to spin and I thought I was going to faint again. With a great effort, I hauled myself up and tried to concentrate. Beside me, Mum began, for what seemed like the hundredth time, to list my symptoms.

'She's got a constant headache and a sore throat; she faints when she tries to do anything; her glands are swollen and look – her finger nails have turned blue just from sitting in the waiting room!'

Dr Passford smiled nervously and made a stupid joke about NHS waiting rooms not being the most conducive to health which was kind of missing the point: I mean, I hadn't seen anyone else's finger nails turning blue back there. She did examine my glands, though. Then she sat back tapping the end of her pencil against her front teeth, clearly trying to puzzle it all out.

'I wonder,' she mused, 'if this isn't one of those post viral illnesses. Let me see . . .' She swivelled her chair round to face the computer again and started to scroll through more pages of seemingly baffling information.

'Yes. You certainly did have a heavy viral load when I first saw you, back in March.'

'What is this illness?' Mum asked.

'Post Viral Fatigue Syndrome. I have to say, I don't know a lot about it myself but there is someone who deals with these cases. Hang on a minute . . .' She grimaced as she prepared to do battle with the computer yet again.

I felt relief flood through me. Post Viral Fatigue Syndrome. I had a name! I wasn't on my own anymore. Now, surely, somebody would have to *do* something.

Dr Passford typed and clicked for a few minutes, nodding occasionally as new information popped up on the screen.

'That's it: Dr Stoke,' she announced in triumph. Then she turned round to study us both closely, almost nervously, before adding, 'She's a psychiatrist.'

'No way!' I cried. What was going on here?

'There's nothing wrong with her *mind*,' Mum said. 'It's her *body* that's not working right. You've felt her glands, seen her finger nails. I mean, she can barely sit up, for heaven's sake!'

'Yes, I understand,' Dr Passford smiled sympathetically. 'But these post viral syndromes are very complex illnesses with no single cause or definite cure. Dr Stoke is really very good. She has a lot of experience with these cases. In fact, I believe, she's helped many people recover quite quickly.'

'But how can a psychiatrist cure a headache?' Mum asked.

'It's obviously not quite as simple as that.'

I was confused. Surely it *was* as simple as that. I just wanted someone to take the pain away so I could get back to normal, back to myself.

'As I say,' Dr Passford went on, smiling valiantly all the while, 'I can't offer you a magic cure but what Dr Stoke can do is teach Sarah how to manage things on a day-to-day basis. It's just that, sometimes, some people need a bit of extra help to push themselves out of these illnesses or they can spiral downwards. At the very least, it must be a very stressful time for you and

40

your family and she'll be able to offer you the support you need.'

'Is there really nobody else who can help us?' Mum asked.

I couldn't believe it; she was starting to agree with Dr Passford. She actually thought I needed a psychiatrist. Thanks a lot, Mum!

'Dr Stoke really is the most experienced specialist we have in this field.'

Mum looked at me uncertainly, 'Sarah?'

I shot her a frosty stare and then shrugged. I wanted to argue but I couldn't think straight; my brain was all muzzy and I couldn't find the right words. What was the point, anyway? They'd obviously already decided. There was no way I was going to get out of it. If I disagreed, I'd only have to sit here longer while they talked me round and I knew I just couldn't do that, not without fainting again and I didn't want to slip back into that dark, fearful world. I'd deal with this psychiatrist thing later. Right now, I just had to get out of here. I think I would have agreed to a head transplant if it had meant getting home to bed just one minute sooner.

My legs were so wobbly, I had to lean on Mum to get back to the car. I arched furiously away from her as we trudged stiffly side-by-side back through the narrow brick alleyway and across the busy car park. Why hadn't she stood up for me, made Dr Passford see I didn't need some psychiatrist, rather than just agreeing to everything she said?

Neither of us spoke.

When we reached the car, Mum silently deposited me on my side and began walking round to her own. It was almost beyond me to open the door which seemed to have tripled in weight during the hour we'd spent at the doctors. I thought, for one humiliating moment, I was going to have to call her back to help but, just as she turned the corner of the bonnet and half looked back to see if I was all right, it finally gave. I wrenched the door open and crawled into the car. Reaching out and closing it again sent tendrils of pain up my arms. Mum, on the other hand, slid into the driver's seat without even thinking about it. She had a distracted air. Her mind was clearly somewhere else.

I clipped my belt on and slumped forward, my head resting against my knees. That seemed to bring her back to the present.

'Please *try* and sit up a bit,' she begged.

'I can't!' I snapped. 'My head hurts too much.'

'I know but it'll hurt even more if we have an accident and you're like that.'

'Doubt it! After all, I'm making it all up, aren't I?'

'Nobody thinks that, Sarah.' Mum's voice sounded shaky and for one awful moment, I thought she was actually going to cry. She didn't seem like my mother then, the confident, decisive person I knew. *She* wouldn't have caved in to Dr Passford but this woman beside me: frightened, uncertain and with that constant look of anxiety in her eyes, I barely recognised her.

'I know you're upset about this psychiatrist thing.' She sat there ringing her hands in her lap as she spoke. 'Believe me, I'm not that happy about it, myself but we desperately need help and if this Dr Stoke's the only one who can give it to us, then we're just going to have to go with it, aren't we? I mean, when we get there, she'll see you don't need a psychiatrist and then she might refer us on to someone else. I just need some advice: I just don't know what to do anymore . . .

'Anyway,' she went on briskly, suddenly seeming to reach a decision, 'let's get you home to bed. You'll feel better when you've had a rest. You always do, don't you?'

She brushed her hair purposefully out of her eyes and put the key in the ignition. Just for an instant, I saw my mother again, strong and sure of herself. She turned to me and asked, 'Would you like me to stay with you, this afternoon?'

'What's the point in asking? You know you can't take any more time off work.'

'Forget all that. I'm asking you if you *want* me to stay with you.'

'I'll be fine. Stop fussing, can't you?'

I knew I was being horrible but somehow, I just couldn't help myself. I didn't know what was happening to me. If Mum was changing, then I was too. I mean, I'd always been pretty even-tempered, easy going, I guess, but the past few weeks, I'd snapped at everyone. It was like I had some sort of permanent PMT. I felt miserable and irritable all the time and every little thing grated on my nerves. I might have said it was simply being stuck in bed all the time but my mood got worse, not better, when I tried to do stuff. At this rate, I really would be needing a psychiatrist! I took a deep breath and tried to get a grip on myself.

'Really, I'll be fine. Thanks.'

I smiled at Mum and tried to haul myself up a bit so she wouldn't worry so much. After all, none of this was her fault, I suppose.

Chapter Six

Two weeks later, I found myself sitting on a threadbare but comfortable chair in Dr Stoke's office. The room was pretty shabby, like it hadn't been decorated since sometime in the 1980s. In the corner lay a pile of beaten up old toys, so chewed and manky looking that only a very disturbed child would *want* to play with them! Before me sat a low table with a box of tissues delicately placed in one corner. I looked across at Dr Stoke, wondering just how many of her patients she reduced to tears.

She certainly didn't look very threatening. She wore a lot of make-up but it was smoothed generously over her features, not slapped on war-paint style. She smiled a lot and the faint scent of her perfume filled the room. It made me feel sleepy and relaxed like the incense Ali and I had tried out a few months ago. Her hair was tied up in an intricate top-knot which fascinated me. I found myself gazing at it as she jotted notes in the spiral bound folder perched on her lap.

How did she manage to tie it up like that? As I became iller, it wasn't the big things people did, like climbing Everest or running a marathon, that amazed me but small things, like this. How on earth had Dr Stoke found the energy for all those twists and clips? How had she managed to hold her arms above her head for long enough to do it without fainting? I could barely achieve brushing my hair these days and washing it had become a major ordeal that left me drained and weak. Standing in the shower sent shooting pains up my legs and Mum had now insisted on standing sentinel outside the bathroom, with the door ajar, just because I'd fainted last week coming out.

Still, I'd been resting up a lot since seeing Dr Passford and I was actually feeling a bit better. My brain was sharp and clear again, almost back to normal, or at least it was until Dr Stoke started asking all her questions. I was all right to start with. I mean, I could answer the first few fine but then I started to get muddled. A hundred blurry thoughts buzzed in different directions through my brain and I couldn't seem to put anything in the right order. Dr Stoke smiled encouragingly throughout, like each garbled response was a little gem of wisdom. Perhaps this was how all her patients talked.

I sighed. How was I going to prove I didn't need a psychiatrist if I couldn't even string a sentence together?

'So,' she asked as my last pathetic response trailed off into silence, 'how long is it now that you've been away from school?'

Panicking, I looked down at my fingers and tried to count the weeks but I couldn't seem to stop the numbers slipping out of reach. The noise of an express train screeched through my ears and I could feel a tight band of pain across my forehead.

Dr Stoke smiled. 'Never mind,' she said, like being unable to count to ten was the most natural thing in the world. 'Let me see . . .' She looked at her notes. 'That'll be nine or ten weeks now. How do you feel about school, Sarah?'

'S'all right,' I shrugged. I mean, how does anyone feel about school? It was pretty dull most of the time but it did kind of beat sitting in your room, staring at the same four walls, every day.

'And that day you tried to return, a few weeks ago. How did you feel, then? Were you worried about going back, about catching up with all the work . . . maybe fitting in again after such a long absence?'

'Well, I wasn't *before* I went back but when I got there I couldn't understand anything the teachers were saying and . . . and, it was more than that. I just couldn't seem to concentrate, get my brain into gear. There was so much noise and it was like I'd never noticed it before. I mean, everyone in the class was just *really* loud: scraping their chairs a-and shouting all the time. It gave me a headache and made me feel sick and achy and then Miss Freeman – that's the maths teacher – she started going over all the stuff I'd missed and it was like none of the numbers made any sense and then I started to panic . . . and . . . and I felt really ill . . . a-and that was when I fainted.'

Dr Stoke looked sympathetic. 'That sounds like a very unpleasant experience for anyone to have. Does it make you nervous about going back again?'

'Y-yeah, I guess it does. I mean, it was so horrible, the fainting and stuff and I'm really scared it'll happen again. And it's like you were saying. How am I going to catch up on all the stuff I've missed if I can't even think straight?'

'And how are you feeling generally at the moment?'

I started to go through my endless list of symptoms, yet again: the sickness, the headaches, the pains in my arms and neck, the sore throat, the dizziness, the hot flushes. Half way through, I paused and looked across at Dr Stoke. She was nodding and smiling but in a sharp, slightly impatient way, like when you're waiting for someone to finish all the irrelevant stuff and cut to the chase. I faltered.

'Yes, I see but how do you feel you're coping with life at the moment? I mean, is there anything worrying you?'

I blinked. Was this meant to be some sort of a joke? Of course there was something worrying me! My body was falling to pieces, my brain had given up and my life was in shreds! I wasn't exactly going to be jumping for joy, was I? But Dr Stoke was still staring at me intently. She obviously expected an answer.

'Yes. I feel ill all the time. I don't know what's wrong with me and I just want to feel better, get back to normal, you know.'

'Of course,' Dr Stoke smiled. 'I think we'll bring your mum back in now and discuss how we can make that happen.'

A few minutes later, Mum was perched nervously on the edge of the seat beside me. Dr Stoke had settled back down into her chair and was grinning across at us like we were her star pupils.

'Please don't look so worried,' she assured us, looking mainly at Mum. 'I've seen dozens of cases like Sarah's and I can honestly say that all of them who've followed my advice have made a full recovery. In fact, one of them is currently on a cycling holiday round France and she was much iller than Sarah when I first saw her!'

'Really? That's certainly reassuring,' Mum said, looking anything but reassured. 'I suppose we feel like we're floundering round in the dark. Nobody's been able to tell us anything, except that it's some sort of post viral illness.'

'Ah, yes,' Dr Stoke sighed, 'the post viral blues.'

'But what does that actually mean?'

'You see, most of us, when we have flu or a bad cold, might go to bed for a few days but then, when the infection's passed, we get up again, go back to work or school and get on with our lives. For some people, though, and I've found this is particularly true of young girls, all sorts of worries and anxieties – depression, school phobia, problems at home – come to the fore and can get in the way of the normal recovery process. In Sarah's case, I can see, she's a very sensitive child who finds the hustle and bustle of school life difficult to cope with and worries about keeping up with her studies.'

Mum stared at me doubtfully, clearly trying to identify the sensitive, conscientious child she'd just acquired.

'Is it true? I mean, you've never had any problems at school before.'

I looked vaguely from Mum to Dr Stoke and back again. I didn't know what to say. I couldn't work it all out. It was like all the normal thoughts and processes in my brain had just closed down. I felt like something was going wrong somewhere and I should stop it but I didn't know how.

'I don't know. Sort of, I guess.' I slunk back into my chair and hoped they wouldn't ask me anything else. There was a pain throbbing behind my eyes. It radiated out across my forehead. I couldn't cope with the headache *and* think at the same time!

Mum looked sceptical but Dr Stoke was clearly satisfied.

'You see, when this happens, it's easy to get into the habit of not doing things. The most important thing is to get back into a normal routine as soon as possible. For Sarah, of course, that means going back to school.'

'School! Do you really think she's well enough? Last time we tried they were scraping her off the floor! She was in bed for a week!'

The expression on Dr Stoke's face froze and just for a moment, something hard flickered behind her fixed smile; Mum had clearly dropped a few notches in her star pupil billing.

'I do understand,' she replied with a show of patience. 'Sarah's been ill and given you a nasty fright but the problem is, in cases like this, the whole family can get into the habit of treating the young person like an invalid. It's a natural instinct, of course, to protect your child but unfortunately this just reinforces the cycle of inactivity and deconditioning, which can make the problem much worse.'

'I'm not saying she's an invalid or anything but she is ill,' Mum protested and yet again began to list the infinite catalogue of my symptoms. 'Her throat's sore. You can see it's red when she opens her mouth and her glands are swollen. I can tell she's got a headache from her eyes and she can barely keep her food down.'

Dr Stoke nodded patiently. 'I think you've misunderstood me. I'm not denying the very real pain Sarah's suffering but you see, the mind and body interact in ways we're only just beginning to understand. The tests from your doctor clearly indicate that there's no organic – that is physical – cause for these symptoms, so we have to look at other ways of getting Sarah back to normal. I know it's hard to understand but I really do have a lot of experience in these cases. What you have to ask yourself is, is what you're doing at the moment working? Is Sarah getting any better staying at home?'

'Not really,' Mum sighed. 'It's up and down, you know. She's OK for a few days. Then she tries to do something and has another collapse but she *is* better when she stays in bed and rests for a while.'

'Unfortunately, that's half the problem. Because all the normal messages between the brain and body have become so messed up, the brain gives out signals to rest for no real reason. If the sufferer gives in to them, they'll experience immediate relief but in the long run, the body just gets used to doing less and less. Deconditioning sets in, the muscles become gradually weaker and the young person finds it harder and harder to perform any activity at all. They start to find that they need increasing amounts of rest simply to stave off the symptoms. On the other hand, if you over-ride these false messages and get back into a normal routine, the body becomes used to this and gradually stabilises.'

I'd slumped so far down into my chair I didn't think I'd ever get out of it again. Lethargy spread through me. I seemed to be in some sort of a trance. I breathed in Dr Stoke's perfume and followed the rhythm of her voice like the tune of the Pied Piper. Somewhere deep down, under the exhaustion and fuzziness, I suppose I did feel uneasy about what she was saying but I wanted it all to be true so badly. After months of illness, of continual fear and doubt, I was exhausted. Finally, right here in front of me, there was someone who knew what they were doing, who seemed so sure they could lead me out of this nightmare. All I had to do in return was be the person Dr Stoke thought I was, the person she seemed to want me to be, a nervous wreck who couldn't cope with the commotion of normal life and had got herself into a state over school. All I had to do was get myself back there. And how hard could that be? After all, I'd been going to school nearly every day of my life, hadn't I? And I was out of bed right now, wasn't I, sitting here, in this consulting room? This woman was a doctor. If she thought I'd be fine, then surely, she was right, wasn't she?

Mum seemed to be coming round too. 'Do you really think it's the right thing for her, to go back to school? I mean, has it worked for your other patients?'

Dr Stoke nodded, her smile back on full beam now that we were all on side again.

'I'm afraid I can't promise you it's going to be easy. The messages between Sarah's brain and body have become so muddled that her symptoms may even get worse for the first few days but if you ignore them and push on, she'll soon start to feel like her old self again. At any rate, the longer she stays away from school, the harder it'll be for her to ever return. It really is your only option. I'll tell you what,' she said, sneaking a look at her watch, 'why don't you try it for two weeks and then come back and see me, let me know how you're getting on?'

Mum looked at me and I knew, this time, it would have to be my decision.

I took a deep breath. 'I'll try, I guess. After all, I've got nothing to lose.'

Mum nodded, forcing a smile but that wary, uncertain look in her eyes was stronger than ever. She was biting her bottom lip as she got to her feet and helped me haul myself up.

I walked slowly out of the room, looking down at my feet, trying to concentrate on putting one in front of the other. Behind me, Mum hesitated, half turning, as though she wanted to say something but Dr Stoke put a reassuring hand on her arm and guided her gently through the door.

'Don't worry!' she murmured in an undertone I obviously wasn't supposed to hear. 'It's always young girls who get these things and they pull themselves out of it, soon enough. You just have to be firm and keep giving them a push in the right direction.'

Chapter Seven

We'd come to resemble an elite army corps on special manoeuvres. Ali stood in the hallway by the front door, her black hair scraped back into a tight plait, wearing that look of aggressive determination usually reserved only for maths lessons. She reached out a hand to open the front door and jerked her head back to look at Mum.

'Ready?' she demanded.

Mum nodded grimly. She stood in position by the hall table. Her fist clenched the car keys so tightly that the whites of her knuckles showed. She had the strained look of someone trying to hold the world together, single handedly, as the plates it rested on drifted relentlessly apart.

She turned to face me.

'Ready?'

I sat on the bottom stair, gazing hopelessly down at my untied shoelaces: I was not ready.

Dr Stoke had said that it would get easier as the

days went by, that we'd get back into a routine but all we seemed to have achieved was this regimented hell.

Monday morning hadn't been so bad. I'd rested up all weekend and the sheer thrill of leaving the house for something other than a doctor's appointment had buoyed me up and carried me through the pain. Mum'd driven Ali and me to school as my legs were still pretty weak but all the same, you know, I was doing all right: I got myself through the noise and commotion of registration and made it to geography over the other side of the school with just a few little rests on the way. I even managed to look like I was paying attention as Mrs Wallace began a tedious description of Brazil.

I felt OK until halfway through the lesson when the fog of pain and nausea gradually started to descend on me again. The sensations were familiar enough but their sheer intensity was alarming. The hard plastic of the chair pressed against the base of my spine sending shooting pains up my back and neck. I battled against them but gradually felt my upper body slouch down onto the desk as, one by one, my muscles gave up the fight. I smelt the disinfectant and plastic of the table top and scanned the classroom. Me and Ali were sitting in the second row from the back with only Steve and Johnny and a couple of other boys behind us. Before me, the rest of the class sat sprawled across their chairs, looking bored apart from Chloë who was busy passing notes back and forth with her friend Sophie. She wrote something and glanced across at me. Then, catching my eye, looked away quickly. She wasn't gossiping about me again, was she? Mind you,

I didn't much care. I just wanted to know why I was the only one whose neck no longer seemed able to hold their head up!

Wallace was pacing up and down, droning on about Brazil's exports but I could see she'd clocked me out of the corner of her eye. She's one of those people who doesn't believe in illness and thinks a brisk jog at six in the morning is the answer to all life's problems. She doubles as a PE teacher. Anyway, somewhere between aircraft parts and coffee, she finally lost her patience.

'Will you sit up Sarah! Honestly, no wonder you kids are always ill. Your posture's appalling! It doesn't do your internal organs any good to be all squashed up like that!'

I wrenched my head reluctantly upwards, resting it on my clenched fists while every muscle in my neck screamed with pain.

Beside me, Ali put her hand up, her face a mask of innocent curiosity, 'Is cancer caused by bad posture, then, Miss?'

'Don't be stupid, Alison!' Wallace snapped.

Ali muttered something under her breath about the distribution of stupidity in the room; I just tried to stay focused on getting through to break when I'd arranged to meet Dan but the lesson stretched before me like the ever-lengthening corridor of a nightmare. Soon, Dan became a vague memory and all I really wanted was to lie down. When the bell finally rang, I let my head drop onto the desk for a few moments before dragging myself back up again. Then I shoved my books hastily into my bag and squeezed past Ali, who, ruler in hand, was turning to Johnny and Steve to berate them for their "disgraceful posture".

'See you at lunch time,' I whispered.

'Don't do anything I wouldn't do,' she called after me as I joined the throng to get out of the classroom.

Excitement and adrenaline kept me going. Well, they did for the first half corridor, anyway. After that my legs went all shaky and it took me ages to reach the steps by the boiler room where I'd arranged to meet Dan. Long enough to remember what I'd overheard Chloë saying at registration: 'She's such an attention seeker! Dan must be getting well sick of it all.'

Was she right? I mean, Chloë usually knew about a fifth of what she thought she did but I hadn't actually seen Dan for more than two months now. We spoke on the phone all the time but he always put off coming to see me. I'd got a bit annoyed about it but hadn't worried too much because I always figured I'd be better any day and everything'd sort itself out. But maybe he *was* sick of waiting. Maybe, I thought, with a sudden plunge deep in my stomach, he'd been so keen to meet up this morning just so he could dump me.

But as I rounded the corner to the boiler room, I knew instantly that, as usual, Chloë was talking rubbish. Dan sat on the bottom of five steps that led up to a little used side entrance. It was a rare, quiet corner mainly because no-one could ever work out if it was off limits or not. There was probably some rule but I don't think even the teachers knew what it was and as long as you weren't smoking or fighting or unlucky enough to run into the caretaker in a bad mood, no-one really cared.

Anyway, Dan was sitting there, bent over his bag, trying to look all cool and casual. He was leafing through his books, lifting one out and dropping it casually back again, pretending he hadn't seen me, that he hadn't been looking out for me but he had this goofy grin all over his face that I knew had absolutely nothing to do with the history book he'd just picked out.

I covered the last few yards between us with a final spurt of energy born of relief and flopped down beside him. I was completely shattered and hoped he wouldn't notice how much I was sweating. It felt like I'd just run a marathon!

'Interesting book?' I asked nodding towards the history of medicine he had in his hands.

'Oh yeah,' he smirked, dropping it quickly back into his bag. 'So you made it, then?'

'Why? Did you think I'd stand you up?'

'Well, you haven't exactly got a great track record. I mean, last time we arranged to meet, I end up getting Ali, in a foul mood, telling me you've collapsed in maths and she hopes Pythagoras is happy now and looking at me like if she can't blame him, I'm the next best thing!'

I laughed, leaning my elbow back against the cool paving of the step above us. 'Yeah, sorry about that. She can be a bit much until you get used to her.'

'That's all right,' he smiled back. 'She sort of grows on you. Anyway, how's your first day back going?'

'OK-ish, I guess. Just had geography. Wallace was her usual self but apart from that . . . Anyway, I'm sick of talking about how I am. It's all I seem to have done for weeks now. Tell me what's going on with you? Did you meet up with your dad last night?'

'Yeah, he took me out to the pub actually. Mum'd have a fit if she knew but Dad keeps wanting to do all that buddy stuff these days like he's making out we're best mates or something when really it's just embarrassing. I mean, we sat there in the pub, at this sad little corner table, not really knowing what to say to each other. And then between one awkward silence and the next, he suddenly announces that he wants me to go up to Manchester this summer and stay with him, you know, after my GCSEs. I can just see the look on Mum's face if I put that one to her! As it was, I had to make out I was meeting up with friends last night. I mean, it's just easier, isn't it?'

He looked across at me but I'd stopped listening. Manchester? This summer? That'd just be typical, wouldn't it, for him to disappear off up north the second I got better and we might actually spend some time together.

'Are you going then?' I asked trying to keep my voice level.

'No way! Not for the whole summer, anyway. I mean, he'd be at work all day and I'd just be stuck in his flat in the middle of nowhere. I'd rather be with my mates a- and you, of course.' He stared down at the drawstring of his bag, frowning with concentration as he tied a particularly intricate knot. 'I-I've missed you, you know.'

My heart did a little leap but I reminded myself he had some explaining to do and wasn't getting off that lightly!

'Yeah, right! So much so that you were just breaking down the door to get to see me, weren't you?'

He looked up. 'You said not to come!'

'What?'

'You said you hadn't exactly told your parents about us and it'd be easier if we just waited till you were better.'

I glared at him. How could he twist things like that? 'That was at the beginning, like when I thought I'd be back at school any day but the past couple of weeks I've kept trying to get you to come round. You *know* that and you've been like "yeah, cool, we'll meet up really soon but I've got football tonight" or "it's my Mum's birthday" or "I've got this really big geography project due" or a million other excuses why you couldn't come round till the next day or the next or the next . . .'

I was building up steam now, ready to explode; Dan looked slightly alarmed. This wasn't like me: I was never hot-headed, hardly ever lost my temper but there again, it wasn't like me to spend two and a half months in bed either.

'Yeah, well, I did have all those things on,' he muttered shifting his gaze back to his bag. He was now trying to unpick the stupid knot he'd only just tied; I folded my arms across my chest and stared mutinously forward. 'I don't know,' he went on, 'It's just all that time in hospital when I was a kid and my parents splitting up and stuff. I guess I'm just not that good at the whole illness thing.'

'Well, maybe I'm not that good at "the whole illness thing" either but I didn't get much choice about it, did I?'

61

I clenched my fists and turned away to stare furiously at the boiler room wall. He hadn't told me anything I didn't already know but just to come out with it like that, like it was some sort of decent excuse for not coming to see me all that time. I was so angry; I could virtually feel the steam rising off me!

And then he was reaching out for me, taking hold of my arms. I felt the pressure of his grasp as he turned me back to face him. I allowed my body to be twisted round but I didn't meet his gaze, just stared straight down at our feet on the paving stones. His fingers felt warm through my shirt sleeves; my heart beat furiously against my chest; my head was spinning. I tried to stay focused, to remember exactly what I was angry about but it was slipping away to be replaced by a foggy haze through which the only thing I felt for certain was the heat of his touch.

'Look, Sarah!' There was such urgency in his voice that I looked up despite myself. 'I'm sorry, I really am. I've made such a mess of things. I guess, I just kept hoping you'd be back at school any day and everything'd be OK, we'd get back to where we were, you know. So I didn't do anything and I know I've screwed up and it's all so stupid because . . . because . . . I *really* like you.'

And then, quite suddenly all the anger drained from me to be replaced by this ridiculously high-pitched joy. What was up with me? It was like my brain had given up and I was running on pure hormones. One minute, I was so wound up, I'd be on the verge of a killing spree and the next, I'd be off on some major high. And over what? A few words telling me what I already knew or could have guessed, anyway. I mean, of course Dan *liked* me or he wouldn't have asked me out, would he? It was hardly a confession of undying love and yet, here I was, forgetting everything, everything he'd done, everything apart from him and the warmth of his fingers against me.

When I finally spoke, I made my voice sound extra stern, trying to hold on to my last scrap of dignity, 'Well, it just so happens you're in luck because I *quite* like you, too.'

That crooked grin spread across his face and he looked so relieved I almost burst out laughing. He kept hold of my arms. I thought he might kiss me but he just sort of held me like that for a few seconds longer and then let go. There was no-one about but we were overlooked by the humanities corridor and I had to admit the thought of snogging in full view of Wallace and co. was a bit of a turn-off.

'Anyway, is all that over with now? I mean, you're back at school so does that mean you're better this time?'

'Kind of, I guess. The doctors have done all their tests and there's nothing wrong with me. I still feel ill but they say it'll be all right if I just keep going and ignore it.'

'Oh . . . er . . . OK.' Dan sounded confused. 'Well, you look good, anyway.'

'Yeah . . . well . . . thanks.' I didn't quite know what to say. I certainly wasn't feeling particularly great and I couldn't understand how it was that I felt like death but looked absolutely fine.

The bell rang for the end of break; I jumped and let out an embarrassing little yelp. My heart pounded out of all proportion to the short metallic buzz. It brought on a fresh wave of nausea but I made myself ignore it and smile reassuringly at Dan so he wouldn't think I was a complete nutter. It seemed to work.

'D'you want to meet up tonight?' he asked.

'Yes!' I nearly blurted out but then I screwed up my eyes and forced myself to be practical: I was already longing for bed and it was only break-time. An evening with Dan on top of my first day back was probably a bit much.

'I don't think I can. What about lunch tomorrow? Mum's working so we could go back to my place or,' I added quickly thinking about the long walk home, 'we could meet up here again. Actually, that's probably best.'

'All right. Sounds good to me,' he said, slinging his bag over his shoulder and standing up; I stayed where I was. 'Er . . . aren't you going to your next lesson?'

'Yeah, of course!' I picked up my bag and pretended to rummage through it. 'I've just got to sort this out first.'

'Oh, Right. See you tomorrow, then' he called as he disappeared round the corner and out of sight.

The truth was I hadn't wanted to get up while he was there. I needed to lever myself up slowly *without* an audience. Also, I couldn't quite remember what direction I was supposed to be walking in. When I did get up, the world span round me, everything ached and each step seemed to require the most enormous effort, like those guys you see on the moon taking giant, uncomfortable looking steps, only in their case it's because there's no gravity and in mine, it felt like the entire universe was pressing down on me.

I trudged painfully on, passing the drama stage where a group of Year 11s was practising a dire sounding play about the dangers of drugs. I rested, leaning against the wall, listening with my eyes closed and praying we wouldn't be forced to watch the whole thing as part of some excruciatingly embarrassing assembly. Finally, I could take no more and forced myself to move on.

By the time I reached the art block, I was seriously late. I walked through the familiar door with its peeling red paint and saw the classroom had been completely re-arranged. Somebody, with a zillion times more energy than me, had dragged the tables together so they formed a circle, in the centre of which sat a bowl of particularly unappetising looking fruit. The class had their pencils and paper out and was busy sketching. Ali wasn't there. She has trouble drawing a stick man and gave up art as soon as she could so I slid silently into an empty space next to Steve who tutted and tapped his watch pointedly, grinning broadly all the while. Ms Thompson had seen me, of course, but she was over the other side of the room enthusing over the texture of a banana, so I had a few minutes to recover before she had a go at me.

I knew I'd be in big trouble for being so late. Thompson and me don't get on all that well at the best of times. When I draw, you see, I like things to look right, to kind of balance each other or at least bear some resemblance to what's actually in front of me. I mean, what's the point of art if you're just going to make everything look all weird and fuzzy? Thompson, though, she's like this total hippy, "go with the flow" type. She bends over my work with this deep frown of concern like she's contemplating world famine rather than just looking at some coursework and then she'll say something like, 'Well, it's very well drawn, Sarah but there's no life in it. The world is *not* symmetrical. Let your imagination loose for a change. You might surprise yourself.'

At which point, I generally mutter a quick 'Yeah Miss' and scuttle back off to my seat before she can slip me any mind-altering drugs.

So I was rather surprised when Thompson came floating towards me in her flowing tunic and long skirt, not just smiling but positively beaming. She crouched down by my chair and murmured in low, friendly tones, 'It's lovely to see you back Sarah. How are things going?'

'Er . . . OK,' I lied.

'Well you just take it one step at a time. These things can take a while to get over sometimes. Now, as you've probably gathered, we're sketching fruit this lesson. Just start when you're ready. We're trying to capture shape and texture. I really want to be able to *feel* the fruit as well as see it in your picture.' And with that, she was gone without a word about my lateness or the fact that I'd missed about a term's worth of work!

'Teacher's pet,' Steve grinned. He'd stopped work unashamedly to listen to our conversation, his pencil hovering above a half drawn orange.

'Shut it,' I muttered absent-mindedly. I was still trying to work out what was going on.

I got my pencil and paper out and looked at the bowl in front of us: the dimpled orange, the blackening banana, the two bruised apples. For a minute or two, I was lost, thinking about how I was going to capture their uneven, mottled surfaces against the shiny reflections of the glass bowl but somehow when I started trying to sketch, I couldn't co-ordinate anything. I tried to draw the oval of the bowl but it came out all wobbly and uneven. I looked down at my hand and saw it was shaking, and up again at the fruit which had gone all blurry.

Beside me, Steve was shading round an orange, biting down on his tongue that stuck out slightly from his still-grinning mouth. Opposite, two girls were whispering to each other until Thompson gave them a sharp stare and they stopped abruptly.

I took up my pencil again and tried to concentrate harder, to draw something, *anything* but after a few minutes, I was forced to give up and rest my head down on the table. I swear, I'd only been like that for two seconds before Thompson pounced.

'Are you OK?'

'Yeah, I just get giddy sometimes. The doctor says I have to work through it, though. I'll be fine.'

'W-well,' she said doubtfully, 'don't push yourself too far; just rest when you need to and Steve . . . keep an eye on her.'

'Yes, Miss.' His voice seemed a little too high pitched. When I raised my head, I saw his habitual grin had vanished; he looked petrified.

'You all right, Sarah? I mean, you were fine one minute and then you kind of went this greyish-white colour and now you just look awful!'

'Thanks,' I muttered putting my head back down onto the desk. 'You really know how to cheer a girl up!'

After a few minutes I tried to carry on drawing but it was no good. I felt sick and dizzy; my body was running hot and cold and I could feel sweat pouring down my back.

'Oh nooo,' I moaned and Thompson, who must have been keeping a pretty good eye on me herself, was by my side again.

'Look. I don't care what this doctor said. You're obviously not fit to be in school, not in *my* class anyway. I'm taking you to Sick Bay.'

I tried to protest but it was all I could do to stay conscious. The trip to Sick Bay was a long one as every few minutes I had to crouch down on the floor to stop myself passing out.

Fifteen minutes later, Mum arrived looking breathless and harassed. When I saw her, I felt relief flood through me and I burst out crying even though I was in school with half a dozen people walking past the open door.

'I'm sorry. I did try,' I sobbed.

'Never mind,' Mum said in a cool, calm voice which contrasted unnervingly with her sharp, flustered movements. 'We'll get you home to bed and see how you are tomorrow.'

Bed! The idea sounded so good. I'd been sleeping sixteen or eighteen hours a day until then. It was the only thing that kept me going. The illness seemed to follow a pattern. I'd try and do something, get sick, collapse into bed, sleep for hours, sometimes whole days at a time, feel my energy levels rising, get up and try to get back to things but then collapse all over again.

I was fairly sure I'd spend the afternoon sleeping and then feel better in the evening but when I finally got into bed, I couldn't settle. It was like the adrenaline I'd used to get myself to school wouldn't leave my body. The events of the morning kept repeating themselves over and over, all the stuff Ali, Chloë and Dan had said running in a continuous loop through my tired brain. I writhed about in bed. When evening came, I felt even worse than I'd done at lunch time. Still, I thought, a night's sleep would set me up for the next day. I'd never had any trouble sleeping before but that night I thrashed about, turning from my left to my right side and back again, over and over. Words and images flashed through my brain non-stop until finally, sometime in the early hours, I drifted into a light, restless sleep full of vivid dreams and flashing lights.

Next morning, I shuffled through school like a zombie. My limbs felt heavy, my muscles cried out with pain and all around me lay the green haze of nausea. I trudged down the ever-lengthening corridor towards the science lab. Only the thought of lunch with Dan kept me going but I didn't even make it to break.

Five minutes into biology and some particularly fascinating diagram of the layers of soil and the room began to swim. Cold sweat flooded my body and again I was falling into that sickening pit of unconsciousness. I gripped the bench and tried to hold on, to stay with the lesson but a few minutes later I found myself coming round on the floor surrounded by scattered books and a jumble of chair, table and human legs.

'At least it wasn't a practical,' Ali muttered as she half carried, half dragged me to Sick Bay. 'You could've blown up half the school!'

Another night of insomnia and strobe-lit dreams followed. And now, here I was, at the bottom of the stairs, on the third morning with Mum and Ali waiting to begin the daily operation of delivering me to, and hauling me round, school.

'Ready?' Mum asked again.

I stared hopelessly down at my shoes. I wanted to follow Dr Stoke's advice, to keep going at school, to be normal again but my body kept letting me down. And now, on top of everything else, I'd forgotten how to tie my shoelaces. I grasped the two ends with determination but the pattern of small, sharp movements necessary to tie them completely escaped me.

Defeated, I crammed them down into my shoes, praying they wouldn't work loose and trip me up: the last thing I needed was to spend even more time sprawled on the floor. I stood up, swaying slightly, and gripped the banister for support.

'Ready,' I murmured to the carpet.

Looking up, I saw Ali's face – a closed mask. I could imagine her clenched teeth behind the thin line of her lips. She reached out a hand to pull the front door open but then, without warning, slammed it shut again and stood with her back against its glass panels, staring back at Mum and me.

'This is stupid! Sarah's not scared of school. I mean, she always gets good marks and she's got loads of friends. She keeps collapsing because she's *ill* and if this doctor's so convinced she should keep going, maybe she could come and pick her up off the floor sometimes because I'm sick of it.'

Ali stopped as abruptly as she'd begun. The silence in the hall hung like a leaden cloud over our heads. Mum turned furiously to Ali and I waited for the storm to break. You see, Mum's got a bit of a temper on her and Ali had just broken all the rules, Dr Stoke's rules, anyway. We were supposed to be ignoring my illness and acting like it would all go away if I just kept going at school. I could see Mum was furious and even Ali, who wasn't usually intimidated, looked a bit scared.

Mum opened her mouth to speak, or more likely, yell, but then shut it again. She stood frozen for an instant before closing her eyes and leaning her head back against the wall. She was now clutching the car keys so tightly that I half expected to see the jagged metal edges cut right through her clenched fist. Without warning, she opened her fingers and let them drop onto the hall table with a clatter that made me wish people could make their points a little less noisily.

When she opened her eyes again, I was surprised to see the uncertain, anxious look, which had clouded her face for weeks now, replaced by a new clarity. She finally looked like Mum again.

'Sit down, Sarah, before you drop.'

I sank gratefully back down onto the bottom stair.

'I'm sorry I put you through this. I knew it wasn't right but that Dr Stoke seemed so sure.' She held her hands out before her, palms upward. 'We had to try it but Ali's right. Any fool can see it's not working. You're ill and you should be in bed, at least until you can stand without collapsing, anyway.'

A rush of emotions swept through me: relief at the thought of bed rather than those endlessly spinning school corridors but also resistance to the very idea of giving up. I wasn't ready to let go of the hope Dr Stoke had offered, the certainty that I could get back to my normal life whenever I chose if I just kept going, if I just tried hard enough. Without that, the illness opened up before me, like an endless pit of fear and hopelessness.

'But I *can't* go to bed! Dr Stoke said I'll never get better if I don't go back to school now. I'll just get more and more behind and then I'll never catch up!' I paused. I could feel myself losing control, tears springing to my eyes. 'But I don't think I *can* go to school. I feel so ill and anyway, I can't write or think anymore and now . . .' I gestured hopelessly down at my shoes, '. . . I can't even remember how to do my laces up!'

During my speech Mum had quietly covered the few steps between us and slid herself in, to sit on the stair beside me. She waited for me to finish before putting her arm gently round me. Then, in the silence that followed, she let out a long sigh.

'Look, I'll tell you what. We'll make a deal. When you've remembered how to tie your shoelaces, we can start worrying about your GCSEs again, OK?'

It wasn't like she meant it to be funny but as Ali walked towards us, she caught Mum's eye and then mine. Her lips twitched; she was obviously trying not to laugh. I clapped a hand to my face but it was too late: the giggle escaped out of the corner of my mouth and rolled over Mum and suddenly, it was like we'd all overdosed on laughing gas. Ali dropped to her knees before us and within seconds we were literally clutching our sides in nervous hysteria, clinging to each other for support as each fresh wave of laughter surged through us. We just couldn't stop ourselves. I don't know what we were laughing at. I mean, it wasn't like anything was particularly funny but I think that was kind of the point. It wasn't funny laughter, you see. I knew that because I remembered it from once before in my life.

I was nine years old and wandering through the lobby of the crematorium on the day of Grandad's funeral. The walls, I remember, were dark wood panels, sombre and intimidating. My parents walked in front of me, Jack, seven years old, tufty haired and freckled, beside me. We looked numbly at the wreaths, all those bleak Rest in Peace messages. Shock and grief rose and fell like waves within me. And then, quite suddenly, amongst those sombre colours, there was a bright bouquet, so obviously a mistake that I was amazed no-one had noticed it before us. It boasted a lividly violet card reading: *Happy Birthday, Darling Debbie!* Suddenly Mum was seized by a convulsive shudder and Dad's face was etched with concern.

'I'll get the attendant to take it away,' he whispered but Mum was shaking her head.

'It's not that.' It was obvious she was laughing now; her voice was nearly inaudible between wild gasps for breath, 'It's just . . . it's just *Darling Debbie's* going to get a wreath for her birthday!'

And Jack and I had joined in her contagious laughter until all the little murmuring groups of aunts and uncles, cousins and friends had stared at us, half scandalised, half confused and Dad had had to lead us all quietly away to the car until we'd calmed down.

We laughed then as we laughed now because nothing was funny because perhaps, nothing would ever be funny again. The world had suddenly become so bleak, had shifted so far from anything we could recognise that we'd somehow lost all appropriate responses to it.

'What on earth's going on down there?'

The voice came from above. We looked up to see Jack, half dressed, leaning awkwardly over the banister. The unfastened tie slipped from his neck. He snatched it clumsily back and noticing Ali, quickly buttoned up his shirt.

'Nothing, love. Your sister's . . . just having some . . . some . . . trouble with her shoelaces,' Mum hiccupped.

Jack stared back at us with that "whatever" look on his face that he seemed to have perfected over the past couple of months. He backed away, muttering something about a bunch of cackling witches which set us all off into fresh peels of helpless laughter.

I can't say all this was the most fun I'd ever had but it was some time out, a break from reality, I guess. When you're rolling about on the floor in hysterics, you don't have to think about what you're going to do next, or how you're going to get through the next week or the next day or even the next hour.

It couldn't last forever, though. Apart from anything else, I didn't really have the energy to do the whole hysteria thing in style. Soon, I was gripping the banister and retching with each fresh wave of laughter, a sound which, take it from me, is pretty much guaranteed to put a dampener on even the liveliest of parties!

'Oh no,' Ali cried, still sprawled on the hallway floor. She dropped her head into her hands to try and calm herself.

'It's all right, Sarah.' Mum's voice was suddenly calm and sober. She put one arm around me and with the other reached out for my cold, sweaty hand. 'You'll be fine in a minute. Just try and breathe deeply.'

Ali raised her head, her face drained of all amusement, 'Look, do you want me to stay, take the day off school? I'm sure Mum wouldn't mind, just this once. I could phone her now to check, if you want.'

Jack, sniffing a day off school at fifty paces, came bounding down the stairs. 'Yeah, maybe I should stay home too . . . to help, you know.'

'Oooh no!' Mum brushed down her jeans and got to her feet to let Jack pass. 'I'm going to be in enough trouble keeping Sarah off school without being accused of running some sort of truancy refuge.' And with that, she reached out a hand to help Ali up off the floor and then started pushing Jack towards the front door. Within seconds, she'd bundled them both outside. Ali called past her that she'd be round to see me after school.

'She'll be fine. She just needs rest,' Mum assured us all. Then, with one firm sweep of her arm, she closed the door and turned back to help me slowly up the stairs to bed.

THE HOLE

Chapter Eight

Weeks passed; I rested. Soon, I could walk to the bathroom again without passing out; a simple conversation no longer made my head spin; I even remembered how to do my shoelaces up!

Mum still had to give up work, though. Her boss made it clear there'd be no more time off. Besides, the strain of balancing work and looking after me was starting to get to her.

As it happened, she had plenty to keep her busy. We'd given up expecting help from Dr Passford. She was sorry we hadn't found Dr Stoke "helpful" but seemed confused about what we expected her to do next. So Mum got back on the Internet. She'd been on it before, of course, but when she'd googled "Post Viral Fatigue Syndrome", the computer had thrown 209,000 results back at her! TWO HUNDRED AND NINE THOUSAND! It'd certainly been a surprise to discover that, despite Dr Passford's confusion, I didn't have some mystery illness nobody had ever heard of. The problem was there'd just been too many results, too much conflicting advice and weird therapies on offer. We'd decided we'd better just do what the doctors said.

Now, though, Mum got back online with renewed vigour, sifting through and researching the links. She contacted support groups, sent for books and pamphlets and spoke to other families who were going through the same thing as us. As well, of course, as running up and down stairs bringing my meals, helping me back and forth to the toilet and filling me in on what she was up to.

By the time I was able to read again, my bedside table, the coffee table, every surface in the house it seemed, was overflowing with leaflets, books, even 500 page treatises – on *my* illness. I felt elated. Somewhere, in amongst all those words, would be the sentence that'd tell me how to get out of this mess.

My joy lasted about as long as it took to pick up the first book. I turned immediately to the section labelled *Recovery*. How long was this going to last? I got a nasty shock. I read it over and over, each time willing the words to shift round, to change their meaning. Then I stared down at the page in blind panic. Only 20% of people got properly better and it took some of them two years! The rest only got partly better and kept having relapses for years and years and if they were really unlucky they just stayed ill, like forever. It couldn't be true; it simply wasn't possible. People didn't just get flu and then spend the rest of their lives in bed, did they?

Mum tried to reassure me. 'You're not reading it right. Those are the figures for adults. It's true, some of them don't do quite as well but, see here . . .' She picked up another book with a luminous orange cover. '. . . this one's for young people and it says they mainly all get better – it just takes time.'

I tried to calm myself but I couldn't forget the first book, that panic, the terror that I might not get better, that this might just be my life from now on.

Through it all, Mum was amazing. I couldn't deny that. We should've been best of friends, what with all the time we were spending together. We were certainly closer but sometimes it felt like we were stuck together with the illness, *in* the illness almost. More than anything, I hated being dependent on her, particularly when we were arguing and I still had to be grateful for her getting my meals and looking after me because I was too ill to do it myself.

At least I still had Ali to talk to, though.

'What's going on between you and your mum? The atmosphere's positively toxic!'

We were in my room: I was sitting up in bed and Ali was on my desk chair, her bag dumped on the floor by her feet. She'd come round to see me after school, only to be caught in the middle of a clipped exchange between me and Mum.

'We had a row about Dan,' I sighed, sinking back against my pillows. 'She said it was really great I had someone but if I wanted to go on seeing him in my bedroom, we'd have to leave the door ajar.'

'What?!'

'Exactly. I mean, it's hard enough having a relationship with someone you can only see for half an hour a day without having to broadcast every intimate detail to the entire house! I tried to explain to her how impossible it'd be—'

'Yeah and what did she say?'

'Aghhh, it was so embarrassing. She just looked at me, straight in the eye, like this, right,' I fixed Ali with a furious stare, 'and said that she couldn't handle me getting pregnant on top of everything else!'

Ali snorted, nearly falling off the chair. 'She doesn't mince her words, your mum, does she?'

No, she doesn't, I thought bitterly. When she'd come out with it, I'd been so angry and embarrassed too. I mean, how would she like it if I started talking about her private life like that? All I'd wanted to do was storm out the house, slam all the doors behind me, get as far away from her as possible. I'd thought about going to Ali's or Dan's, maybe staying out late, just to show her but I couldn't. I mean, I wouldn't even have made it down the front drive without collapsing. So I'd just had to stay put, fuming silently, in my bedroom.

'Still, at least Dan's coming round to see you now,' Ali said.

Yeah, I thought, cheering up a bit. I'd see him again tomorrow. Even with the door ajar, we could still talk quietly and kiss and stuff, as long as there was no-one right outside. And let's face it, there probably wouldn't be. Jack seemed to be on permanent detention and was never home till five or six and, to be fair, once Mum had checked out the door situation, she'd probably just stay downstairs and leave us to it.

Ali stretched back on the chair and gazed over at

my bedside table. It was piled high with a selection of the books and pamphlets that littered the entire house. Mum was trying to get me to read them but, to be honest, I'd lost all enthusiasm. None of them had easy answers and I could still only read a couple of pages before the words got all mixed up and fuzzy so, all in all, it was pretty slow going.

Ali reached forward and picked up one of the books. She flicked idly through it.

'I don't get it. These books are all about Chronic Fatigue Syndrome and ME but I thought you said you had that post viral thingy?'

'It's the same illness,' I muttered unenthusiastically. I'd read enough to know that much. 'Sort of, anyway. Post Viral Fatigue Syndrome becomes Chronic Fatigue Syndrome or ME after three months or six months or something like that. Well, if you don't get better first.'

'What? You go to bed one night with this post viral thing and wake up the next morning with ME?'

'Something like that.'

'Bargain! Two illnesses for the price of one!'

I laughed. The misery I felt over the illness, over the pile of endless books with their boring, depressing details, was still there, somewhere in the background but talking about it with Ali made me feel a bit better. Anyway, while I was sitting here, chatting away as normal, it didn't seem so real somehow.

But Ali was frowning again now, holding the book and scowling down at it puzzled.

'Yeah, but that still doesn't explain why there's two different names for it after a few months: Chronic Fatigue Syndrome *and* ME?'

'There's more than two!' I said with some satisfaction. I actually knew quite a bit about this. The description of the different names usually took up the first ten pages of any book with the author explaining why they were using one term or another and begging people not to have a go at them about it. As page twelve was the furthest I'd reached with any of them, it was actually the only thing I was qualified to talk on.

'There's ME,' I began. 'That stands for Mya . . . Encepho . . . something or other. It's to do with the brain and muscles and spinal cord. Only doctors won't call it that because they say it's not right; they call it Chronic Fatigue Syndrome but that's not right, either because it's not like being tired's my main problem and I certainly don't sleep anymore. I just feel ill and fluey and stuff. And then there's all these old names people don't use much anymore and the Americans call it something different again . . .'

Ali's frown had deepened. She was starting to look quite distressed.

'Look, what am I supposed to call this thing, like when people ask about you at school? I only need *one* name! I mean, what do *you* call it?'

I paused. I'd read all the information like it was some exercise for school, like it didn't really have anything to do with me. I'd never sat down and thought about it before so it took me a minute or two to answer.

'ME, I think. I mean that's the only one that talks about the brain and muscles and those are the bits of me that aren't working right.'

Ali nodded wisely. 'Probably best. It's the only one anybody will have heard of and I don't think Steve or Johnny's brains are up to adding any new information. It'll be better th—'

Ali stopped abruptly, interrupted by the violent slamming of the front door as Jack came in. She jumped slightly and stared in the direction of my door questioningly. I looked at the alarm clock. He was late again. Surely not *another* detention. We sat in silence listening to the stamping of his footsteps across the hall and then the crashing of cupboard doors in the kitchen. It was kind of hard to concentrate on anything else. He was obviously getting himself a snack but it sounded more like a herd of elephants had descended on our house for the sole purpose of making a cheese sandwich.

Ali raised an eyebrow.

We heard Mum come out of the living room to talk to him but could only make out snatches of her voice: '. . . quieter . . . your sister . . . a little consideration . . . once in your life . . .'

Jack's response came through loud and clear, though, 'I'm sick of hearing about it; this whole house revolves around *her*. Well I live here too and I'm not going to—'

Mum's voice, inaudible.

Jack again, 'Oh, just leave me alone!' And then a crashing sound as he dropped whatever he was doing and stormed upstairs. I winced as he smashed his bedroom door closed.

Ali frowned and picked up another book, clearly trying to find something to cover the awkward silence that had fallen over the house.

She needn't have bothered because within seconds Jack had put his music on at a deafening volume. The noise vibrated through the thin partition wall that separated our bedrooms.

'You're kidding me!' Ali said. 'I thought my sister's taste in music was bad but this stuff's positively Neanderthal!'

I smiled weakly. The room rocked in time to the heavy beat of the bass; I was starting to feel a little seasick. I closed my eyes but that only made the dizziness worse. Ali had leaned closer to the bed and was saying something about my birthday but I couldn't make sense of the words. My ears were ringing and my head was so full of the thud, thud, thud of Jack's music that nothing else could get through.

Mercifully, the track came to an end and there was a brief silence as Jack searched for another.

'Are you doing anything with Dan on your birthday?' Ali repeated.

I shook my head. 'He's going off to his dad's.'

'What? On your birthday!'

'Well, he wants to get up there as soon as possible after his exams are finished so he can get it over with. Anyway, it's not like I can actually do anything is it? I mean, my eyes hurt so much I couldn't even watch a DVD!'

'Yeah, well, we'll still have a good time,' Ali declared bravely, if rather unconvincingly. Then, struck by a sudden idea, she went on more enthusiastically, 'We can make plans for next year, you know, the joint bash for our sixteenth. You haven't forgotten, have you? I'll come bearing marshmallows and chocolate. That's if DJ Charm in there hasn't finished you off first!' She nodded aggressively towards the wall as the music started up again.

She kept talking but Jack's music zapped all the energy in the room; I couldn't take anything else in. Eventually, even Ali gave up. She got up from the chair in one fluid movement then kicked it carelessly back under my desk. Swinging her school bag over her shoulder, she waved her arm in an exaggerated arch, mouthing a goodbye. Then she was gone, walking purposefully out of my room with strong, healthy strides.

I sank down onto my pillows. I tried putting one over my head to block out the relentless pounding from next door. It filled every corner of the room. My head throbbed in time to its nauseating beat. I really did think I was going to be sick if it went on much longer but it stopped quite suddenly in mid track.

I took the pillow off my head and came face to face with my bedside table and its toppling pile of books. I reached out to steady them but only succeeded in sending them flying across the room. I watched, helplessly, as they scattered across the floor. I felt too ill to pick them up now. I'd have to deal with them later, when I'd had a rest.

As I sank back on my bed, I found myself thinking about Dan and Ali. It was weird, the difference between them. I mean, Ali would pick up the books, read bits, pull faces and ask questions but Dan . . . he just acted like they weren't there. Even when he'd spilt his drink all over them one day, he still didn't seem to take in why they were there or even what they were, for that matter. He came to see me all the time now and we were getting on great. To be honest, he was the one good thing in my life at the moment, well, apart from Ali, but we just never talked about the illness. I told myself it was good that he treated me the same; he still liked me and didn't think differently of me just because I was ill. Sometimes, though, it felt like there was this big hole right in front of us and Dan was tiptoeing round it, trying desperately to pretend it wasn't there, leaving me to look down into the darkness on my own.

But I never felt like that when Dan or Ali was actually here. Some sort of adrenaline kept me going through their visits and chatting away, I felt like my old self. Sure, if they stayed too long, things started to go haywire: words got mixed up, my speech became slurred and I started to feel sick and dizzy. That's why I made sure they only stayed half an hour. I could hold things together for that long, seal up the dark hole that was becoming my life.

It was only afterwards, when I felt tired but unable to rest, with the adrenaline still racing through my veins that the illness became real again. I vanished deep into its pit. It swallowed me whole, leaving no room for anything or anyone else. I became its prisoner with no identity of my own but it was only Mum who saw me then. After a bad night or one of Dan or Ali's longer visits, I would lie in bed, unable to move or rest, pain searing through my muscles, my head aching and my mind racing with unprocessed thoughts and images. She was the only one who really understood what it was like, what I went through, which made it ten times worse when we were arguing.

I was so deep in my own thoughts that I failed to notice how dangerously quiet Jack had become until a knock on my door shattered the peace yet again. I looked up to see him hovering in the doorway.

'Can I come in?' he mumbled.

I shrugged and stared at the ceiling. He seemed to take this for a "yes" and strolled in, crushing several of the scattered booklets underfoot. He plonked himself down on the edge of my bed causing it to rock violently. The sickness rose up in me again. I closed my eyes: if I refused to look at him, he might just go away. But no . . .

'So, how's things?' he asked. His tone was cheery and fake.

'Couldn't be better,' I replied, dryly, wondering where all this was going. At any rate, I decided he obviously wasn't going anywhere till he'd said what he'd come to say so I opened my eyes to get it over with.

Jack was staring at me, conspiratorially. 'Look, you can tell me, you know, if you're faking. I mean, I won't say anything to Mum and Dad. It'd just be good to know . . .'

His eyes were almost pleading, like he was drowning and wanted me to throw him a lifebelt. I glared at him as I felt all the anger and frustration of the last few months build up within me.

'Yeah, right! I'm doing this for a laugh. I just love

89

lying up here with no mates, no TV and no sleep. I mean, do you actually think I *want* to be like this? Great lifestyle choice, eh?'

Jack looked like he'd been hit by an express train. 'I'm sorry. I-I got it wrong. I just thought . . .' he trailed off abruptly as, to his horror, I burst into tears. It was like telling Jack how it was made it all seem suddenly, horribly real.

'I'm sorry. I didn't know. I didn't think. I-I . . .' He reached out and for one awful moment, I thought he was going to try and hold my hand but in the end, he just patted the duvet close to my left arm in an awkward, frightened sort of a way.

'Just go!' I said, trying to keep my voice level.

He got up but hovered uncertainly over me. I turned my face to the wall. '

'Look, Sarah—'

'Go!' I screamed.

He fled from the room, knocking yet another book off my bedside table on his way.

I pulled the bedclothes over my head, curled myself into a ball and wept. I wept until my head throbbed and I could barely breathe through my already inflamed throat. I didn't know how much longer I could hold it all together. I *had* to get out of this house. It wasn't just the illness or the "bedroom door crisis" or even Jack and his music. My whole family was falling apart and it was all my fault. Since Mum'd given up work, her and Dad were at each other's throats all the time. They argued about everything: Dad's work, Mum's lack of work, who was doing the shopping, what insurance to take out on the cars, even whose turn it was to load the dishwasher but most of all, they fought about me.

The night before, achy and sleepless, I'd crawled out onto the landing on my way to the bathroom only to be sidetracked by the sound of them bickering behind their bedroom door.

Mum had obviously been trying to keep her voice down but it kept rising upwards, heavy with anger, 'I'm the one who looks after her when she's throwing up or too weak to even lift a glass to her lips and I can tell you for a fact she's not putting it on and if you think—'

Dad's answers had come in short, irritable bursts, 'For crying out loud . . . I never said she was putting it on . . . Just that we might want to think about approaching this in a different way, pushing a bit harder, encouraging her to do more—'

'Right, well, I'm obviously doing it all wrong. I'll tell you what, as you're such an expert, why don't we swap places? I'd be more than happy to leave this house every day. Maybe I could sit in my little office, away from all the problems while *you* drive her to school every morning and collect her two hours later when she can barely stand . . . We've tried pushing her and look where it got us! Two half mornings at school and she was in bed for a fortnight! It was four days before she could even string a sentence together! Didn't you notice or were you conveniently at work the whole time?'

'Well, somebody's got to keep their job. The bills aren't going to pay themselves just because Sarah's ill! It strikes me, she can manage well enough when it's something she wants to do, like seeing Ali or this lad—'

'*Half an hour!* She manages *half an hour* and then spends the rest of the day getting over it—'

Outside, on the landing, my head had sunk down onto my knees. Their voices had risen almost to screaming pitch. Even so, I'd nearly jumped out of my skin when Jack had suddenly hammered on his bedroom wall.

'Just shut up, can't you?' he'd yelled. 'I'm trying to sleep or is that not allowed in this house anymore, either?'

I'd slipped silently back to bed.

And now, the next day, after Ali's visit and the scene with Jack, I lay there, thinking about it all, wondering if my parents were going to get divorced like Dan's and this time it really would be all my fault. I couldn't bear just lying there with it going over and over in my brain so I crawled gingerly out of bed and started collecting the scattered books and leaflets. Every movement sent screeching pains though my muscles but I didn't stop. I longed to be doing something: I was too keyed up to rest. I placed the books carefully back on the bedside table and lay on top of my bedclothes. The house was quieter now. Downstairs, Mum was preparing dinner. The distant sound of pots and pans clanging against surfaces drifted upstairs. Next door, Jack stayed ominously silent. It was anyone's guess what he was up to.

I heard Dad's car pull up and the front door slam as he came in. What was it with the men in my family and doors? He didn't go into the kitchen to see Mum.

Instead, he trudged up the stairs and went straight to the bathroom. I heard the shower running. Then, a few minutes later, he knocked briskly on my door.

'Yeah?' I mumbled.

He came in loudly, knocking his thigh against the corner of my desk.

'Damn! It's a bit gloomy in here, Sarah. Shall I draw the curtain back some more?' He moved towards the window.

'No!' I cried. 'The light hurts my eyes.'

'Oh, yeah, yeah, your Mum said.'

I clenched my fists. *Then why ask?*

He stayed hovering, agitated and twitchy halfway between the door and the window. When he spoke, his voice was too loud and unnaturally cheerful, like he was trying to fill up all the silence in the house.

'How are you today, anyway?'

I shrugged.

'It'd be nice if you could get back to school and your friends soon and that lad you've taken up with, wouldn't it?'

I dug my nails into my palms. 'Really, d'you think? I thought it'd just be nice if I stayed here for the rest of my life, feeling ill.'

Dad looked surprised and a little hurt. 'All right, Sarah. I was only trying to help.'

'No, you weren't,' I snapped. 'You were, you were, trying to . . . to . . .' I searched for the right words but only found a haze of irritation and despair.

Why did everyone – Dr Stoke, Jack, Dad – think I could stop this whenever I wanted, that all they had to do was push me in the right direction because, of course, it'd never occurred to me that living a normal life might be a tad more entertaining than lying in bed all day?

Dad sank his head into his hands. He looked suddenly old and tired. 'I just want you to be well again,' he sighed.

'Just leave me alone then, can't you?'

'All right, all right, Sarah.'

He sighed again, more heavily this time, defeated almost. Finally, to my great relief, he left, closing the door behind him. He didn't go downstairs to Mum but slipped quietly into their bedroom.

I lay in the darkness. The room around me seemed to be bursting with anger and frustration. Throbbing pain stretched through my body and I was overwhelmed with the sick dizziness that was becoming all too familiar. Through the haze of it all, I was sure of only one thing: something had to change – and soon, before the world I knew finally snapped apart.

Chapter Nine

Actually, things did start to change over the next few weeks, just not in the way I particularly wanted. A few days after my conversation with Dad, he tripped over yet another ME book. Only this time, instead of ignoring it, he picked it up and started reading. He began, sheepishly at first, to ask for more information. Pretty soon he was insatiable; he read everything, particularly the dense, scientific stuff I avoided like the plague. He'd obviously decided to stop pretending the problem would go away and try to solve it instead.

They say ignorance is bliss and there were certainly times when I wished Dad had stayed in denial! Now, whenever I saw him, all he wanted to do was discuss my endocrine system. He was never happier than when he could link my symptoms to specific neurological processes, like some sort of gruesome mix and match game. All of this grew more than a little tiring, particularly as he seemed incapable of getting any sort of a grip on my timetable and had the habit of bursting into my bedroom full of some new discovery just as I needed to rest.

Mum read everything she could get her hands on too but her focus was different: she read to feel less alone; she searched for other people out there like us and found out how they were coping – to get ideas, I guess. Dad read more frantically. He snatched up each new fact greedily. It was like my illness was a puzzle and he thought if only we had all the pieces, we could solve it. He didn't seem to realise that we no longer lived in a world where those pieces stood any sort of a chance of fitting together.

To make matters worse, Jack was acting weird. I mean, weirder that usual! I kept hearing him shuffling about outside my door before knocking lightly. Yeah, LIGHTLY! A bit freaky, eh? Then he'd sidle nervously into my room and mutter,

'How are you doing today?'

I'd answer something non-committal and we'd stare at each other awkwardly for a while until he decided to shuffle off again. That was apart from the day I'd had zero sleep and lost it with him.

'What do you care, Jack? You just think I'm putting it all on, don't you?'

He stared back at me, genuinely surprised and then began to speak very slowly like I was about five years old, 'That was *ages* ago.' It'd actually been the week before. 'Anyway, I never thought you were putting it on, exactly. I just wanted to check, you know. I thought it might just be something to get out of school but it'll be the summer holidays soon and no-one'd be ill then if they could help it, would they? It's obvious, isn't it! What? What you smiling at?'

'Nothing,' I answered quickly. I was actually wondering how come Dr Stoke with all her posh qualifications, couldn't work out something so simple, that it was obvious even to my idiot of a brother!

At any rate, Jack was being nice to me. That could only mean one thing: life was getting seriously out of control. Something had to be done! Since the disaster with Dr Stoke we'd been trying to go it alone, figure things out for ourselves, but it wasn't working.

'I don't get it. I'm pacing myself like the books say but I just seem to be getting worse.'

It was true. I never watched TV or read for more than quarter of an hour. Most days, I couldn't even manage ten minutes and I only saw Dan and Ali for half an hour. I'd even started timing their visits, much to Dan's confusion and Ali's amusement. Dan would stare at the cooking timer in hurt bewilderment like it was that and not the illness that was causing all our problems. I always rested, well more like collapsed, for ages after their visits but it was no good: I still felt ill all the time.

'I know you're doing your best, Sarah,' Mum sighed.

Mum, Dad and I were in my bedroom having one of those heavy discussions that just a few blissful months ago would have been about what time I was coming in but now revolved around doctors and management strategies.

Mum sat perched on the edge of my desk. She'd picked up an eraser from the stationery caddy and was kneading it compulsively in the palm of her hand, frowning down at it all the while. Dad, on the other hand, was pacing up and down the small space in the centre of my room, making me dizzy. It seemed he could understand the most complex processes at work inside my body but was completely incapable of grasping the simple, day-to-day things, like being still and quiet, that would actually help me.

Mum put the eraser down and looked directly at me.

'I think it's time we got you some proper help.'

'No way! If we go back to Dr Passford, she'll just send me to see Dr Stoke again and I can't, I won't, Mum. She doesn't get it at all—'

'It's OK. I wasn't thinking—'

'It strikes me,' Dad interrupted, stopping short in mid pace, 'that a neurological illness should be treated by a neurologist or, given its viral onset, an immunologist.'

'I don't really care who we see,' Mum snapped, 'as long as they actually help us this time rather than just making things worse.'

We all knew what she meant. We'd thought there was nothing to lose giving Dr Stoke's plan a try but the fact was I'd been much iller since. Sure, I'd recovered a bit after resting up but I never got back to where I had been. Before, I could watch TV or read for half the day, walk a bit, sleep at nights. Now my time seemed to pass in a muzzy haze where I couldn't concentrate or do anything but, at the same time, I found it virtually impossible to rest.

'We certainly don't want another shot in the dark,' Mum went on. 'This time we need to know exactly where we're going and what sort of treatment we can expect before we even set out. A lot of people online are talking about this Onslow Clinic. They really do seem to be helping people there.'

'Like making them better?' I asked.

'Not a magic cure but I was speaking to this one woman the other day and she said they'd really helped her with pain control and sleep and explained how to manage the illness.

'The only thing is, we need to get referred by Dr Passford and I don't want you having to go to and fro to the doctors. I mean, it's going to be hard enough getting you to the Onslow Clinic without lots of appointments before then. I wonder if she'd do a home visit?'

But the fierce receptionist, who guarded the entrance to the health centre, made it clear that doctors only made home visits to the elderly or dying or, reading between the lines, people who were *really* ill, not to malingering teenagers with dubious sounding illnesses. There was no way I was making myself even iller by sitting on the hard-backed chairs of the waiting room for hours on end, just to see a woman who wasn't even sure what illness I had so Mum decided to go in on her own. Disappointing though it was, I guessed I'd just have to pass on hearing Dr Passford's words of wisdom for the time being.

When she got back, Mum reported that Dr Passford was the same as ever: still engaged in ongoing hostilities with her computer, overwhelmed with paperwork and completely clueless about ME. Still, she did agree to refer me on. In fact, she seemed relieved to be passing the buck.

It was at that point, back home in my bedroom again, that Mum decided to tell me exactly where the Onslow Clinic was.

'No way! That's like an hour's drive!'

'Mmm,' Dad mused darkly. 'Traffic, you know, I'd leave two hours to be sure.'

Mum glared at him.

'I'm only trying to help,' he muttered defensively.

'Mum, there's no way I can do that,' I moaned. Talking hurt that day. It felt like I was speaking through shards of glass. 'You know how ill I was the other week when you drove me to Ali's and that's only five minutes away!'

Mum came over to sit on the bed and took my hand but I pulled away and rolled over to face the wall. I couldn't afford to cry; I didn't have the energy. Crying burned my throat and turned me dizzy. After the last time, I'd got a rash under each eye where the skin had peeled away for days afterwards. But, as with so much else these days, it seemed I didn't have any choice: the tears came anyway. I lay there helplessly, feeling them scalding hot down my barely healed cheeks. A sob escaped me every now and then and my head burned with the effort of it all.

Behind me, I felt Mum motioning to Dad; he left the room. Stillness returned. Mum was good at being quiet for me. She knew how important it was and her stillness had a peaceful quality to it that Dad and Jack, with their fidgety restlessness, couldn't seem to manage. We stayed there, together in the darkness, for a long time. At some point, my tears stopped and I lay listening to Mum's even breathing.

She reached out for my hand again.

Eventually, I rolled back to face her. I let her brush the tangled hair out of my eyes. It made me feel like I was about five years old but, right then, I was too ill to care.

'I can't take it anymore. I can't do a journey like that. You know I can't but I can't go on like this either. I just feel so ill and I don't know what to do.'

'I know,' Mum sighed. 'I don't know what to do either but I do know that we need help and there just isn't anywhere nearby. Will you give it a go, love? I know it's going to make you ill but I really don't think we've got any choice.'

'All right, all right, I'll do it. Just leave me alone now, OK? I've got to rest.'

She left and I closed my eyes against the world. Reality was becoming too much and I wanted to be left alone to block it all out and dissolve into memory. I thought back to last summer, to sunbathing in the park with Ali, lounging and listening to music with the distant sounds from the tennis courts opposite flowing towards us on the warm breeze. I dreamt of another summer, too: the summer that might have been. In my head, I walked with Dan, talking and laughing, the sun pouring down on us as we linked hands. And then, in the twilight, we kissed, shielded by an avenue of trees with their great overhanging branches.

Chapter Ten

By the time my appointment at the Onslow Clinic came round, I wasn't exactly in the best mood to start facing reality again. It'd been a nightmare few weeks. To start with, I'd had another bad patch and for a while I wasn't even able to see Dan or Ali. I rested, *again*, and soon I managed to get myself back to feeling halfway human.

Of course, the first thing I did was get straight on the phone to Dan. He was a bit iffy to start with, all sort of moody and like "Oh, I haven't heard from you for a while," like I'd been off round town enjoying myself with my mates, not stuck in bed, feeling like death, for the past fortnight. Still, he came round in the end and that was when I told him about Saturday. Everyone'd be out and maybe, he might just like to pop round . . .

You see, Mum and Dad had this big family wedding on. Even Jack was being dragged along, moaning all the way. Mum hadn't been sure about going, what with me being so ill but I persuaded her I was much better; I'd be fine on my own; I'd enjoy the quiet. Besides, I made out, Ali might come round and it'd be nice for us to be able to chat in peace for a change, wouldn't it?

Mum looked doubtful and a tad suspicious but I knew it'd be all right. The wedding was this major family do and there was no way she was going to miss it. Come Saturday though, it still took ages to get her out the front door. She was in mother hen mode, flapping about endlessly. Was I sure I'd be all right? Yes, but was I *really* sure? She could stay if I wanted her to. No? OK, but she'd leave her mobile on. I was to phone if I felt at all funny . . . She only finally left when I told her she was giving me a headache and that they'd miss the beginning of the service if they didn't hurry.

Anyway, after that, everything went according to plan. I even managed to spruce myself up a bit: changed my pyjamas, splashed myself with water *and* dragged a brush though my hair. By three o'clock, I was safely tucked up under the covers, with Dan. All right, so it wasn't exactly the great romantic setting I'd been dreaming of but it was something and it was with him.

We were lying there, talking and kissing and stuff, having a pretty good time actually when my body let me down, yet again! OK, so maybe it wasn't quite that sudden. Maybe there'd been warning signs, even before Dan'd arrived, like nearly fainting when I tried to force the brush through my hair and finding it hard to stand to put my pyjama bottoms on. I just thought if I ignored it and pushed through, then the illness might let me have this one afternoon. It seemed only fair after all that time resting but I should have known it didn't work like that.

'I'm sorry,' I gasped, 'I've got to stop. I don't feel very well.'

He didn't reply. Well, not unless you count grunting as some alternative form of communication. We'd been kissing, his hands stroking my neck and back, our legs wrapped tightly round each other but when I said I wasn't well, he pulled right away from me. Pushing the covers back, he got out of bed and flopped down onto my desk chair. I curled into a ball, my knees in the warm space where his body had been just moments before. I waited for the sickness to pass; he straightened his clothes and stared moodily down at the floor.

'There's no need to be like that!' I snapped when I could speak again. 'It's not like I'm doing it deliberately. Or maybe you think I am, like that doctor I saw!'

He looked up, startled. 'It's not that. It's just, I don't know why you asked me here. I don't know what I'm supposed to do, what you even want from me.'

And what *did* I want? The answer was simple: I wanted everything, everything that had been possible just a few months before. I wanted to go out to the cinema, to walk in the sunshine, to kiss under the trees. It wasn't much to ask but he couldn't give it to me, nobody could.

Everything was falling apart and I didn't know how to pull it back together again. I curled up tighter, hugging the covers round me for comfort. I didn't want to become a blubbering mess again particularly not in front of Dan but I couldn't seem to stop myself.

'Oh, don't cry, Sarah. Look, do you want me to go?'

And looking at him through the blur of my tears, I saw that was exactly what he wanted: to leave this house and all its problems behind but he wasn't brave enough to admit it. He wanted me to release him, to give him permission to go, to say, "Yeah, I'd really love to be left on my own, feeling like death, thanks. That's probably the best thing you could do for me right now." Well, I wasn't in the mood to make things easier for him. If I had to suffer, then he could too, just for one afternoon.

So I stared up at the ceiling and refused to answer and we just sort of stayed like that, not talking, our breaths catching in the empty space between us. After what seemed like an eternity, I turned and saw my bedside clock with its hands at half past four.

'You'd better go now,' I shrugged. 'They'll all be back soon.'

He got up, looking relieved and left the room without a backward glance. 'Well, see you then,' he mumbled as he closed the door behind him.

And since then, I hadn't heard from him so I didn't even know if we were still going out. Going out? That was a joke! I mean, when was the last time I did that?

Ali came round a couple of days later. I didn't tell her about Dan. It was just that I always got the feeling she didn't rate him that highly to start with and just then, I couldn't bear to hear her tearing strips off him.

I mean, I could be as angry with him as I wanted but no-one else had the right. They didn't know him like I did, didn't understand what was going on between us.

As it was, I could hardly get a word in edgeways. Ali was ranting on about her sister nicking her favourite top, you know, the one I'd worn on that date with Dan. Don't get me wrong, it was great to see her but she was so worked up that she kept forgetting about needing to be quiet. Her voice filled the room, rebounding off the walls and piercing into me. After she'd gone, I lay there, my head pounding and my ears ringing. Dan and Ali's visits were my only relief, my one break from the illness but now it seemed even they were too much for me.

So you can imagine what sort of a mood I was in by the day of my appointment. My life was over; what did it matter what some doctor said now?

Around me Mum and Dad (well, mainly Mum, to be honest) scurried about preparing provisions fit for a ten-month voyage: fleeces, blankets and hats to combat the shivering cold I felt even in August, snacks to keep my brain working and a bulky assortment of sick bags, painkillers and ear plugs. I lay on the sofa watching it all happen and wondering how on earth I was going to make the journey.

Jack was being left behind with strict instructions not to trash the house, make too much noise or burn down any neighbouring buildings. Leaving him "home alone" was a safer option than it would have been a few months before: he'd changed recently, grown up, I guess. Admittedly, he was still ridiculously lazy but as it was now the summer holidays this no longer landed him in constant detention. He spent most of his time out, like he couldn't bear being trapped in the house with its dark, heavy silences. I didn't blame him. Given half a chance, I'd be first out the door.

When he was in, he'd become noticeably quieter. Sure, his footsteps still sounded like a herd of elephants trampling round the house, but he didn't slam doors anymore and I hardly ever heard his music. The weird thing was, now it was gone, I actually missed it. It was like one more link to normality had been severed. I longed, more than anything, to get back to how things used to be, with me hammering on the wall and yelling at him to turn his music down and him turning it up louder, just to wind me up. I needed peace to rest but sometimes, the silence around me seemed as much of a prison as the illness had made my body.

The journey to the hospital was worse than I even expected: I slumped in the back of the car, the seat belt cutting into the skin of my sagging neck; I spent most of the time with my head in a sick bag; my hands and feet felt icy cold; at one point, I started to faint. I really thought I might die, there and then, on the M-whatever-it-was motorway, with the asphalt rolling remorselessly on beneath me.

When we finally got to the hospital, I took my belt off and sunk down across the back seats. I lay like that for some time. Eventually, my body stopped churning and I could manage one of the snacks Mum'd brought. I felt a bit better after that, well enough to face the next part of the day, anyway.

107

Dad drove the car round to the main entrance and Mum helped me into the wheelchair she'd borrowed from the Red Cross. I hadn't been worried about using it before we set out. I mean, it was logical, wasn't it? I couldn't walk very far and a wheelchair was just another method of transport, like a car or a bicycle – or so the ME books said but when I actually came to it, I felt my whole body tighten. Embarrassment and self-consciousness surged through me. As I lowered myself into the chair, a girl my age watched idly from the bus stop opposite. Two women smoking cigarettes on a nearby bench, stared at me intently but they didn't see *me*, not the girl who joked with Ali, the one who was good at maths and drawing, the one who shivered when Dan ran his hand down her spine. To them, I was just an extension of the wheelchair, something interesting to fill a dull moment.

"Just another method of transport, like a car or a bicycle," I repeated to myself but it wasn't the same; I felt exposed in a way, I was fairly sure, no cyclist had ever done!

As we swept through the automatic doors into the hospital, the noise hit us like a blast of hot air. The foyer was packed with shops selling flowers and cards, toys and clothes. It felt more like a busy shopping centre than a hospital. A dizzying multitude of people swarmed round the various reception desks. The whole expanse buzzed with energy zapping activity. How did anyone cope with being ill in a place like this?

Mum hovered uncertainly by the entrance but then, catching sight of a sign for the Onslow Clinic, she began to cut a path through the crowd.

'Sorry. `Scuse me,' she muttered, edging forward.

People smiled or scowled as we passed. Some of them glanced at the wheelchair but thankfully, most were too busy dealing with their own problems to pay much attention to us.

We weaved in and out of one unit after another: Gynaecology, Orthopaedics, Cardiology, each with its own dizzying burst of activity. As we moved deeper into the hospital, we came across little pockets of ominous silence, shut doors at the end of corridors where the signposts ran out, the sort of sterilised, white stillness you'd expect to find in a hospital but which made me shiver, none the less.

By now, I was glad of the chair. We must have covered a good half mile before we finally reached the Onslow Clinic and I was too ill to care what anybody thought. My head and neck muscles ached so much that I'd slumped right over in the chair. I was bent double with my chin resting against my knees.

We arrived at a deserted lobby and were just wondering if we'd found the right place when a flustered looking woman about Mum's age came round the corner. She was balancing several bundles of photocopies with limited success. In fact, she was so distracted that she didn't even notice us till the last minute.

'Oh!' she started. 'Sarah Nelson? Mrs Nelson?'

We nodded.

She looked at me, taking in my state, 'Oh dear, bad journey? You'll be wanting to lie down. I'll just set up the camp bed in the stationery cupboard, OK?'

I was too ill to appreciate the sheer bizarreness of

this comment and Mum seemed too stunned to speak so we followed her, in silence, photocopies scattering to the left and right, as she led us into a pokey little room where she set up the promised bed.

'You'll all be wanting a hot drink, too, I should think.'

She returned five minutes later with tea, coffee and Dad who'd been off parking the car. She'd found him wandering the corridors looking for us.

'We're all on lunch at the moment,' she explained, gesturing towards the empty corridor, 'but Dr Arnold'll be back soon. It's half an hour until your appointment, isn't it? I'll leave you in peace to rest till then. Oh, by the way, I'm Joan, your support worker. I'll be sitting in on your appointment. Then we'll be going over some pacing and management strategies.'

'Th-thank you,' Mum finally managed to stutter. 'It's nice to meet you.'

To be honest, we were all a bit stunned: finally someone medical seemed to understand what I needed.

Half an hour later, Joan led us down the corridor to Dr Arnold's office.

'Come in, come in,' he greeted us. He was quite an old man but had about fifty times more energy than me. He was currently frowning down at a blank DVD, struggling with its cellophane cover.

'Got it,' he announced, easing the plastic off one corner and unwrapping it. I winced as the crackle of it screeched through me.

'Sorry, not a nice noise, is it? It's just I like to record my appointments so you have something to take home with you. It's so hard to take everything in while you're here. Let's face it, concentration levels aren't great at the best of times with this illness and after you've had a long journey . . . well . . .' He slid the disc into a battered, old computer on his desk then smiled broadly, clearly pleased he'd managed the deeply technical operation!

'Anyway, sit down, please.' He gestured towards the scattered chairs but then, turning to look at me, added, 'or would you find it easier to lie down on the couch, over there?'

I stared at him. I was beginning to wonder if all this was some sort of a trap just to see how easily I gave in to the illness, how hard I tried to keep going. I shook my head firmly.

'I'll be fine,' I lied, getting out of the wheelchair to sit in one of the worn, cushioned seats on offer. For once, it took Mum a bit longer than me to settle as she was carting round an array of plastic bags full of our provisions. She flopped onto the chair beside me and arranged them round her feet. Dad, to my intense embarrassment, took out a pen and notebook. He obviously didn't trust Dr Arnold to get a working DVD out of that worn out computer.

Joan, who'd gone off to look for an extra chair, came back with a plastic folding one which screeched noisily as she opened it. I closed my eyes in despair. Would it never end? I mean, with all this fuss and commotion, I might as well be back at school! Finally, though, just when I thought my head was going to explode, the scraping and shuffling calmed down and everyone was ready.

'Right, well, let's get started then, shall we?' Dr Arnold asked from the other side of his cluttered desk.

Mum and Dad nodded enthusiastically; I tried to get my brain into gear.

'I've read through the questionnaire about symptoms and the like that you filled out at home. I know it's rather long. It's just I've found patients have significant difficulty remembering details during the actual appointment so it helps to have something in front of me . . .'

I sat there listening to the hum of the computer, its remorseless drone. It made me wonder what it might be like to be a machine and never get tired. Somewhere, far away, Dr Arnold was saying something, something important about me.

'. . . I think, basically, there's no doubt this is Chronic Fatigue Syndrome or ME. It seems to have started with the stomach bug you picked up back in March, when you had the vomiting and bowel disturbance . . .'

Excellent, I thought. We'd only been here two minutes and we were already into my bowels. I remembered how fussy I used to be about what Mum wrote on my sick notes. "You can't write stomach upset: everyone'll know I've had diarrhoea!" But now, I just didn't care. My symptoms had been trawled over by so many people that this guy could discuss the inner workings of my bowels to his heart's content and I didn't even bat an eyelid. It was like my body was laid out on a slab for anyone to examine, like it didn't belong to me anymore. Or, at least I thought, as I felt the relentless pounding against my head, I wished it didn't.

I turned my gaze back to Dr Arnold, willing a focused look into my glazed eyes.

'. . . Now, as you're probably aware, there's no diagnostic test for this illness, no simple blood or urine sample that can determine whether you have it or not. In the face of this, we have to look at symptoms . . .'

I studied the wastepaper basket with its metal rim, so like the ones at school. I wondered if I'd be able to reach it if I needed to be sick. I thought I probably could but Joan's shiny leather shoes were rather in the way.

'. . . the criteria I use simply states that you should have at least four of the following symptoms (without signs of any other illness, of course): impairment in concentration, muscle pain, new headaches, unrefreshing sleep, post-exertional malaise (that is feeling bad after exercise), sore throat, swollen glands and multi-joint pain. You clearly have all eight of these symptoms!'

Eight out of eight! Congratulations, I thought: it'd been a while since I'd got full marks in anything.

'. . . In addition to this, you also have lots of other symptoms that you'd expect to find with this illness: problems with temperature control, cold hands and feet, pins and needles; you don't like bright lights and you're very sensitive to noise.'

Dr Arnold paused; I snapped back to face him. He was beaming across at me, a satisfied look on his face.

For one awful moment, I thought I was going to laugh and I knew if I started, I wouldn't be able to stop, like that day on the stairs with Mum and Ali. There was just something so disconcerting, comic almost, about this man's enthusiasm for the illness that was ruining my life.

'Now, you're going to ask me what's causing all of this.'

I nodded gravely and tried to form my face into the expression of someone capable of asking such a logical question.

'Well, I think we really are starting to understand much more about this illness in terms of what's actually going on. The evidence coming to the fore is building up a picture of a multi-system breakdown. To start with, things are going badly awry in the brain itself. For example, blood flow to the brain is reduced. Now, your brain needs a tremendous amount of blood to function and if it's not getting it, the bottom line is, it's not going to work right.

'The Autonomic Nervous System also seems to be affected. Now, this is about the body running and organising itself. So, if this goes wrong, you can get changes in heart rate, palpitations, irritable bowel type problems, sweating attacks, disturbed sleep, poor temperature control, thirst, mood swings: one minute you're laughing, next you're crying. You're irritable and tearful. Yes?' He looked at me questioningly.

I tried to make sense on his words: tear-full – full of a tear: I imagined myself trapped inside an enormous tear drop. 'Yeah,' I answered dimly. 'Th-that's right.'

114

'Your adrenal response malfunctions. Patients report that it gets switched on too easily and won't clear from the system so you can't relax after an activity and your body's spending long periods in its super alert fight-flight mode which, of course, has its own knock on effects.'

His words buzzed about me like a fly. No, like a bee, a bee buzzing merrily round the honey pot of my illness. To be honest, I hadn't really taken any of it in since my outstanding eight out of eight score for physical incompetence. Dad, on the other hand, was lapping it all up, manically scribbling into his notebook.

Mum looked irritably over at him before turning to Dr Arnold. 'Yes, all right, that's all very interesting but is there anything we can actually do about it?'

'Absolutely!' He was clearly delighted by any show of interest. 'You see, I believe if people can learn to manage activity, they really do increase their chances of recovery. At the outset of the illness, patients often follow a boom/bust pattern. Everyone's achievement driven: we all want to do things. So, if you get a good day, you push it just a bit too far: you overdo it. That exacerbates all the problems with adrenaline, blood flow and brain symptoms. So the next day you're flat out.

'The basic approach, we recommend here, is to break activity down into manageable chunks and intersperse that, throughout the day, with good quality relaxation sessions so you get into a sort of a pattern. Joan'll help you with that in a minute. Many patients find that once they're "crashing" less, the illness becomes more stable and they can start to do a bit more.

'In addition to that, we really need to work at improving the quality of Sarah's sleep. We have a number of medications that might be worth a try . . .'

Without warning, the seemingly endless flow of words stopped and Dr Arnold looked directly at me. 'You're not taking any of this in, are you?'

'Sorry, I, er, no . . .'

But Dr Arnold just beamed and gestured towards the computer. 'Don't worry. It's all being recorded. You can listen to it when you're back home. Once you've had a rest, your brain'll start to feel a bit better again.'

I stared at him, dumbfounded. After months of feeling alone and scared, finally someone seemed to understand my illness. I felt tears prick behind my eyes; it was all too much. 'Look, could I lie down on the couch now, please?'

'Of course,' Dr Arnold nodded cheerfully. 'That's what it's there for!'

Joan helped me over to it and even found a blanket. Before she went back to the others, she put her hand on my arm and flashed me a reassuring smile. She was so kind. I was glad her nice new shoes were out of my vomit range.

After that, I just lay there, feeling the pain rage through me. I longed for darkness, quiet and rest but the conversation droned on. Dr Arnold continued in the same enthusiastic tones but I caught only the occasional meaningless word: neurotransmitters, hypothalamus, endocrine system, mitochondria . . .

Honestly, I had to have the most boring illness imaginable. I'd been glad, all those months back, to have a name, anything to make sense of what was happening to me but now I was beginning to wish I'd been given any other diagnosis, no matter how awful, rather than this dragging, complicated mess of an illness. I screwed my eyes up against it and tried to rest but all too soon, the appointment was over and it was time to move again, back to the stationery cupboard.

'What's happening now?' I asked blurrily as Joan closed the door on us.

'You rest a minute,' Mum said. 'Joan'll be back soon. Then we'll be going through your timetable.' She produced a large chocolate bar from her bag. 'Here, eat this; it'll give you energy.'

I took it dutifully. My glands grated against each other as I chewed and the chocolate scraped painfully down my throat. I swallowed the last chunk and then collapsed back onto the lumpy camp bed.

Opposite me, Mum and Dad were sitting on the hospital's hard, plastic chairs. Their faces were bright, hopeful almost. I found it hard to share their optimism. I was too busy concentrating on each breath, on getting past the pain and through to the next second. Still, the chocolate did its trick. By the time Joan came back, I was running on a hyper-alert sugar burst: I even managed to sit up a bit.

Joan squeezed herself into the now crowded room, clutching a fresh bundle of papers. Mum and Dad stood up and flattened themselves against the wall so she could edge past them and reach the small table on the other side of the camp bed. The pokey little cupboard of a room was obviously never meant to hold four people, much less a fold-down bed but Joan didn't seem to register any of this. She just plonked her papers down on the table and turned back round to face us.

She pulled out a photocopy of the sheet I'd filled in at home about my daily activities and started to go through them. It seemed we'd got it all wrong. We thought I'd been following a rest/activity timetable because I'd do something major and then collapse back into bed for a few hours but apparently, it wasn't supposed to work like that.

'The idea is that you do small, manageable activities, within your limitations and then rest regularly: maybe half an hour's rest for every hour you're up. That way, the rests become peaceful relaxation sessions, time for your body to recharge its batteries, not the complete collapses of the boom/bust pattern. That's what we're trying to avoid here.'

'What does manageable activity mean, though?' Mum asked.

'Well, it's different for each person, depending on what level you're functioning at. It's trial and error really. The best place to start is by looking at what you're actually doing at the moment and how that's affecting you.' She looked down at my timetable. 'I see here, you have your friends round for half an hour at about four o'clock but that pretty much wipes you out for the evening, doesn't it?'

I nodded.

'Well, how about seeing them for quarter of an hour instead. That way you might be able to do

118

another activity later on rather than just feeling ill for the rest of the day. The same with television. Here,' she pointed to the notes we'd made, 'you watched for ten minutes but then you were too ill to see your friend that day. Why not try reducing that to five minutes or even two?'

I stared at her, 'You mean I get better by making my life even worse?!'

'Sarah!' Mum snapped but Joan just laughed.

'It's OK. I felt exactly the same when I saw *my* first timetable. If I'd been up to it, I'd have run a mile!'

I was confused. *Her* first timetable? I looked at Joan in horror, convinced I'd stumbled across some new age cult. Obviously everyone here had to follow one of these soul-destroying regimes as some sort of exercise in discipline imposed by the manic Dr Arnold.

Thankfully, Mum's brain was working better than mine.

'You had ME?'

'Still do, unfortunately but I'm about 75% recovered now, mainly through pacing. I work here part-time – three afternoons a week.'

I studied her closely. She looked normal; she wore nice clothes and make up. I didn't worry about her only being 75% better or just working part-time. All I knew was, she could do stuff; she looked like she had a life.

'How long?'

She understood my question immediately. 'Well, it took me five years to get to this stage but it might not take you so long. Lots of people your age recover almost completely in a year or two . . .' She saw the horrified look on my face and quickly added, '. . . sometimes sooner.'

None of them seemed to understand. They were all happy to talk about me getting better in a few months or a few years but I needed to be well in a few weeks if I stood any sort of a chance of getting my GCSEs. What was I talking about? I had to sort things out with Dan right now! They didn't seem to realise that in two years it'd be too late. My life'd be over. What'd be the point of being well, then?

'What you've got to remember,' Joan went on, 'is that this low level of activity isn't forever or, even hopefully, very long. We're just trying to get you out of this boom-bust cycle. We have to find a baseline you can do every day without causing a relapse. You won't get rid of the symptoms altogether. I can't promise you that but we should be able to reduce the relapses and hopefully find something to help you sleep. You'll feel much better about everything once you've got more control of your life again. Take it from me, it really does make all the difference.'

Yet again, I found myself wondering what I had to lose. I was seriously unenthusiastic but I couldn't feel any iller than I did at that moment. Besides, if I worked really hard, I might get better quicker, like Joan said happened sometimes. I tried to think through the throbbing and whirring of my brain, tried to form some resolution: I *would* get well and *soon*! Now I knew how to go about it, nothing could stop me.

On our way out, Joan loaded us up with the DVD of our appointment with Dr Arnold and bundle upon bundle of photocopies: guides to establishing a regular sleep pattern and information booklets on everything from brain chemistry to pacing. In short, all the stuff we could have done with months ago when this started.

'You go home now and have plenty of rest for a couple of days. Let your system recover from the journey here. Then start the new timetable. If you've got any questions or you just want a chat, give me a ring, OK?'

Chapter Eleven

But I didn't recover from my trip to Dr Arnold, not in a few days or a few weeks. I was like a spring that had been stretched out of shape: this time, I didn't bounce back. I lay in bed, a heap of raw meat, my brain a throbbing mush of feverish thoughts. I couldn't read or write or even watch TV. My curtains remained shut tight against the autumn sunlight and I learnt that pain doesn't go away simply because you can't bear it anymore.

'You'll be OK in a few days,' Mum kept repeating but as the weeks passed, the hope faded from her eyes.

I was too ill to bear the bouncing energy of Dan or Ali. I got Mum to ask them not to come, not that Dan was exactly making a beeline for my door as it was. Dad exhausted me, too. He sighed and shuffled in the chair by my bed, darting mournful, pitying glances at me, like I was on the verge of death. Soon the pain grew so bad, I couldn't bear anyone in the room except Mum. She'd bring my food up and sit quietly in the darkness for hours on end but even she couldn't manage complete silence. I could feel her writhing with guilt beside me. She'd pushed me to go to the Onslow Clinic, told me everything'd be OK and couldn't forgive herself for the way it'd all turned out.

'I'm sorry,' she whispered into the darkness. 'We had to go, though, didn't we?'

I didn't reply: I wasn't able to. My throat was so swollen I couldn't even swallow, let alone speak, but I begged her to stop with my eyes. Any noise, any emotion, in fact anything but perfect stillness and silence, exacerbated the pain beyond endurance: I couldn't cope with Mum's guilt on top of everything else. She realised this and the tortured questions stopped, at least out loud, but over the next few months, deep lines etched themselves into her face and a streak of white shot down her auburn hair. By Christmas she looked ten years older.

She phoned Joan constantly, desperately. Joan was always calm and soothing. 'This can happen sometimes. After people have been following a boom/bust pattern for a while, their bodies can reach the point where they simply crash. She will pull out of it, though . . . in time.'

But nobody could say how long.

There was no relief, not even at night, especially not then. I lay awake, hour after hour, sinking only occasionally into fluey nightmares that wore me out even more than the sleeplessness which surrounded them.

I tried the pills they'd given me for sleep at the Onslow Clinic but they made my muscles twitch all night; I couldn't lie still and my brain whizzed wildly. I thought I was going mad; my heart pounded so hard it felt like it was about to explode and panic surged through me. Mum was frantic.

'It *will* pass,' Joan assured her, yet again. 'That's the trouble with this illness. Drugs often don't work the way they're supposed to, even on the very low doses we've given you. She's probably best off the pills for the moment, though,' she added, rather unnecessarily.

She reckoned the best thing I could do to recover was rest but also try tiny activities, like sitting up for two minutes or having a crack of light showing through my curtains, just small things I could build on as I felt better. It sounded like good advice but it was too much for me. After only thirty seconds sitting up, I felt so sick I couldn't eat for the rest of the day and even the slightest ray of light gave me excruciating headaches.

It seemed I'd fallen off the scale of what even a specialist ME clinic thought was normal. One of the books they recommended said to imagine that a healthy person had £1000 worth of energy to spend each day, while someone with ME only had £100 and had to decide very carefully on their activities because if they overspent, they made themselves worse. Nowhere, though, did it tell you what to do when you only had £10 worth of energy and it took £20 just to wash and eat.

Actually, the answer's quite simple: you just stop washing!

There was this girl in my class called Sophie. She had a subscription out to every daft magazine you could imagine which might not have been so bad if she hadn't believed every single word she'd read in them. One day she'd tell us that breast implants were made out of cows' stomachs and the next, that we should cover spots with toothpaste to dry them out overnight. Well, she reckoned that if you didn't wash your hair for six weeks, the natural oils revitalised it and you'd end up looking like something out of a shampoo advert. Dream on, Sophie! Back on planet reality, the most that can be said for the whole experience is that after a month or so, it simply doesn't get any worse.

I found myself plunged into a completely different life where I suddenly had to cope with daily impossibilities I'd never have dreamed possible in an underworld I had no idea existed. While I'd been going to school and hanging out with my mates, stepping over puddles and soaking up the sun, others had been struggling for years in this deep, dark hole that had claimed me and they were the only ones who could help me now.

Mum spent half the day on the Internet, getting help and advice from them and their carers. When I became too ill to chew solid food, they sent her dozens of recipes for soups and liquidised meals full of calories which stopped my weight dropping too low. They also told her not to worry about baths and showers: the amount of energy and pain involved made them counter-productive. Instead, they told her to get a damp flannel and wash just one part of my body (say an arm or a leg) each day. That was all I could bear. I found any sort of touch or movement painful beyond belief but at least that way, over the course of a week, I got a basic wash.

One of them even gave Mum an ME information pack for our GP. She passed it on to Dr Passford but I'm not sure she ever read it. Mum visited her regularly, more out of desperation than because she actually expected her to help.

'It's so hard,' she complained to Mum, 'when you come across an illness like this that's not fully understood and you don't have a cure. Everyone expects you to know what to do but you just don't!'

I don't think it ever struck her that it wasn't exactly a bundle of laughs having the illness either. Mum asked her about home visits and she did come out to see me once but having her in my room, talking and expecting me to answer, took up so much energy and made me so ill that we didn't press for more visits. There was nothing she could do, anyway. Nothing anybody could do but wait.

Or so we thought. We soon learnt differently. The news of my illness spread and before long the cure for ME was waiting for us round every corner. It was posted regularly through the letter box or handed directly to Mum by a virtual stampede of neighbours and friends. They were all convinced by newspapers, magazines and the Internet, that they'd beaten the scientists to it and found the cure for my mysterious illness.

To begin with, we tried everything: antioxidants, antidepressants, anti-fungals, antibiotics, pro-biotics, vitamins A, C, E, B1, B6 and B12, fish oil, evening primrose oil and ginko biloba along with a legion of homeopathic remedies to boost my immune system, blood flow, thyroid and adrenal glands.

Our medicine cabinet came to resemble a small chemist's shop. Its contents might have alarmed even the hardest of drug dealers. Jack later joked that he could've made a fortune if only Mum had let him sell the stuff at school! He might as well have done for all the good it did me. Nothing worked. It seemed miracle cures were for other people. The best that could be said in my case was that some of the side effects were so severe that coming off the drugs actually made me feel a bit better in comparison.

Mrs Wilson, our next-door neighbour, proved particularly persistent. She was this kind old lady who used to give me and Jack sweets when we were little. Now, she seemed to devote her time to finding ever more bizarre cures for my illness. Every week, on her way down to the shops, she'd knock on our door with some new suggestion. She never did understand our reluctance to try circuit training or seaweed baths!

The kindness of many friends and neighbours dried up abruptly when I failed to respond to their remedies. Some of them seemed to take it as a personal insult and decided that I was deliberately refusing to get well. One of Mum's friends even suggested she was pampering me by bringing the few slops of food I could manage, up to me, in bed.

'Get back to work. Leave her to fend for herself and you'll soon find she's popping downstairs to make a snack when she's hungry. Then you've got to pack her straight back off to school. No arguments. I know it's hard. I've had it with my own kids. They're always whining about tummy upsets when there's a maths test but you have to be firm or these things just escalate, don't they?'

Of course, I didn't know anything about this at the time. I lay cocooned in layers of pain, barely able to take in the names of the different medicines I was trying, let alone anything else. It was only much later, when I noticed our Christmas card list had been slashed in half and Mum had to explain why she wasn't talking to half her friends, that I got the full details.

I guess people just didn't want to face the fact that an illness like this could fall from the sky onto anyone. As long as they convinced themselves there was something we had or hadn't done to bring it about, then they could go on living in their safe little worlds, where things like this didn't happen, not to them or their children, anyway.

And the weird thing was, in my head, I was doing much the same thing: trying to re-arrange the world back into an order that made some kind of sense. I scanned my feverish brain, searching for the moment when it had all gone wrong and rewriting my life from that point on. If only I hadn't followed Dr Stoke's advice; if only I'd waited a few more weeks before going back to school; if only I hadn't got sick in the first place but just locked myself away for two weeks while that stupid bug did the rounds. I gasped at the simplicity of it, how easily I might have escaped all this: just a few days shut away in my bedroom and the illness might never have found me.

I tried desperately to block out reality: the tortured look in Mum's eyes, the white streak in her hair, my own never-ending pain. I lived in a fantasy world where none of this had happened. I was the old me, not this sickly imitation. I went to school with Ali, joked with Johnny and Steve, rolled my eyes at Chloë's pathetic sniping and Dan was always there, at the end of the day, waiting for me.

When I grew tired of that, I drifted into memories of the world as it had been, of Ali and me at a party, laughing into our spiked glasses of lemonade, of Dan in a school corridor, his hair flopped over his eyes, smiling that lop-sided grin of his . . . and then . . . bam – something would distract me – Mum bringing my food in, the slamming of a car door, the scream of a child on the street outside – and I would find myself dragged savagely back to reality and each time the jolt of realisation, the unbearable misery and longing, would grow that bit sharper.

The truth stared me in the face but I couldn't accept it. There was part of me that even while I lived with the illness, every hour of every day, still believed it couldn't be happening, not to me, anyway. It simply wasn't possible.

And yet it went on happening.

Christmas came and went: a pity card from Dan, an enormous teddy from Ali and the unbearable crackle of wrapping paper, setting every nerve of my body on fire. And downstairs, a world away, I heard the scraping of plates, the murmur of voices and then Jack bounding upstairs, impatient to try out his new game.

Easter barely registered except that Mum tried to feed me melted chocolate as a treat. I threw up everywhere. I was sure I'd never eat another Easter egg again!

More unbearable pain-ridden months and it was summer and the shock that I'd been lying there for a year, a whole year; my class at school had taken the GCSEs I'd barely begun. And Dan, where was he now?

I seemed to have lost my connection with that other world, the world of health. I could sense it all around. It drifted towards me in the smoky smell of a summer barbeque, the noise of children playing in the street, the sound of Dad's car as he returned from work or Jack's heavy footsteps on the stairs. It felt so close: I should have been able to reach out and touch it, grasp it tightly and haul myself up out of the hole I'd fallen into but I was separated from it by the unbreakable barrier of my own body. I didn't feel part of the world any more. Somewhere, during those dark months, I'd drifted so far from health that I'd lost all expectation of it, the belief that one day I'd wake up refreshed, my head clear and my body free from pain. And the more hopeless I became, the more I retreated into my fantasy world and away from the dismal reality that surrounded me.

And so, my sixteenth birthday finally arrived. I refused to spend the day trapped inside the matted mess of my body, in a room with the curtains tightly drawn against the sun. In my head, I set out for the party Ali and I had planned for so long. Everyone was there, laughing and dancing. Steve did his John

Travolta impression and Johnny spiked the punch so that we all swirled round the dance floor, faster and faster, wiping tears of laughter from our eyes. Then the slow songs began and I clung tightly to Dan, knowing I'd never let him go.

THE CLIMB

Chapter Twelve

OK, so I guess you're waiting for the bit where I summon my last ounce of energy, fight bravely back and am miraculously rewarded by a full recovery. Well, sorry to disappoint you, but it ain't gonna happen like that. People have this image of young people who are ill as little beacons of light whose courageous struggle inspires all those who come into contact with them. Well, in case you hadn't guessed it by now, I wasn't exactly cut out for the little angel of light bit and as for the courageous struggle, well, that's a joke! I mean, when the ME got really bad I just sort of folded, didn't I, floated off into la-la land.

By the summer of my sixteenth birthday, I'd just about given up. All I could see before me was day after day of this horrible, dragging illness but strangely enough, it was at that point that I started to get a bit better.

I don't mean I woke up one morning feeling great, jumped out of bed and hot-footed it over to Ali's to catch up on the latest gossip. I just noticed that my life was slowly growing that bit easier. My staggered crawls to the bathroom became less painful, I could bear dim light, I managed to sit up for a few minutes and eat solid food; the vibrations caused by Jack running up and down stairs didn't make me feel like throwing up anymore; I even managed a bath!

That first bath felt so good. I lay there, relaxing, with my eyes closed. The water flowed over and round me, like a warm, comforting blanket. I imagined it washing my body clean, draining the illness out of me and sending it spiralling off down the plug hole.

If only it was that simple but the next day I felt like death. My neck throbbed from being held upright for so long. From my head down to my toes, everything ached, like I'd been in some street brawl, not enjoying a nice relaxing bath!

Things went up and down like that a lot and my mood fluctuated wildly. On a good day, I felt elated; the future seemed so bright: finally, I was getting better. Soon, it'd all be over and I'd be able to go back to normal, to my old life – start a college course with Ali, catch up in no time. Then I'd try and do something normal like watch TV or wash my hair or even just talk to Mum for a few minutes and, in no time at all, I'd collapse back in bed. The next day, the ME would rear its ugly head again, like the monster returning for one last scare at the end of a horror film. On days like that, I felt iller than ever, my whole body screaming out in protest. Worse still, I'd sink into despair and convince myself I'd never be free from the grips of this illness, never get better.

Reluctantly, miserably, I began to understand about pacing. I couldn't just do stuff automatically, like I had before I was ill. I had to learn to live within carefully planned segments. Mum's cooking timer came back into play. I used it to regulate the short sessions I was able to sit up or have the curtains drawn back. When I stuck to it, it did help even out my symptoms but I found it hard to be so disciplined. Even after all those months in bed, I still wasn't ready to let go of my old, easy life. All too often, I ignored the timer and just kept going but I usually paid for it the next day.

Even with these setbacks, there was no denying life was getting easier. I stalled, juddered and staggered towards improvement. By autumn, I was able to bear Dad and Jack in my room again, if only for a few minutes at a time. I never thought I'd be glad to see my idiot of a brother again but, strangely enough, his visits became the highlight of my (admittedly not exactly scintillating) day. He'd come in and see me for five minutes when he got in from school. My brain was clearest round then and I could just about follow his jerky, rapid speech.

It was all a bit weird at first. I hadn't really seen Jack for over a year and he'd changed so much in that time. He'd grown about a foot taller and his freckles had been replaced by a layer of spots. He was really awkward, too, at least to start with. He'd shift from foot to foot, darting nervous, side-long glances at me, like he wasn't quite sure who I was anymore. We tiptoed round each other for a while but it didn't take long for us to start getting on each other's nerves again. One day he trod on my old teddy bear. He clutched his foot and swore loudly; I grabbed the bear and examined the damage to its eye, muttering under my breath and pretty soon we were sniping at each other again, like the last year had never happened. Well, almost anyway.

We never talked about the illness. Instead, Jack would fill me in on what was happening at school. I enjoyed that. It was like some sort of connection to my old life had been kept open but it made me feel a bit sad too because part of me knew that it wasn't really *my* life anymore. It was Jack who was in Year 10 now, where I'd been when I got ill. My year had left school in the summer. Even if I got better tomorrow, I'd never be going back there. I thought about the textbooks and locker key in my desk drawer. I knew I should give them to Jack to return but somehow, I couldn't bring myself to hand them over, to let go.

I felt an aching sort of longing sometimes when Jack talked about school which was pretty stupid because when I'd actually been there, I couldn't wait to get out of the place. Mainly, though, I just enjoyed hearing all the ridiculous stories that were doing the rounds, like the one about the Year 11 boys who got suspended for sniffing glue down by the garages, which just happened to be overlooked by the Staff Room. *Smart!* And the rumour that Ms Freeman and Mr Smith had had sex in the stationary cupboard, with 9C sitting, listening on the other side. *Yeah, right, very likely!*

And then there was Mrs Pryce. I remembered her. She was a supply teacher, one of those shaky, nervous types, you know, the sort everyone's really glad to see because they know they're just going to be able to ignore her and chat all lesson. Well, according to Jack, one day she completely lost it. She gave up trying to shout instructions over thirty screaming teenagers. Instead, she stood silently gazing out over the class with one of those mad smiles on her face, like teachers get just before they're about to lose it big time. She'd stood frozen like that for ages until finally this ominous silence had descended over the whole class. Then she'd laughed. Yeah, laughed! Well, more sort of cackled apparently, like some mad witch or something.

'You know what,' she'd said to the stunned class, 'I don't *have* to be here. I don't have to do this every single day. There has to be more to life than this.'

And with that, she'd just walked out and no-one had seen her since.

I thought about that a lot – what it might be like to walk out of your life. I wished I'd done it, that night at the cinema with Dan, taken his hand and run as fast as possible, away, out of my life, simply not allowed the future to happen. To where though? And to what? And anyway, you might be able to walk out of your life but you have to take your body with you and I was already ill by then. Perhaps there never had been an easy way out of this or maybe the only way out was the long, tough haul through it.

At any rate, those few snatched moments with Jack became gradually easier and pretty soon, perhaps too soon, I decided I was up to seeing Ali again. I wanted to phone her myself and hear her familiar voice at the other end of the line but the phone had become an alien instrument. My mobile sat in my drawer, tucked away with my school books and locker key. I still wasn't too good at putting numbers and letters together and even if I'd actually managed to press the right buttons and get through, I don't think my brain would've coped with a stream of disembodied words catapulting themselves towards me. So I got Mum to do it while I lay upstairs, waiting impatiently.

Five minutes later, Mum walked into my room, smiling broadly. 'She's coming round today: four o'clock, straight after college. She's really excited you're up to having visitors again. Says she can't wait to see you.'

Today!!! I felt suddenly, unexpectedly, alarmed. I mean, Ali and I had been such good friends, always doing stuff together but how would we get on now? What would we talk about? I looked round my dimly lit room with its discarded bottles of painkillers and its frozen, stale air. I had nothing, nothing anyone would want to hear about, anyway. There was no way to get out of it though. I knew from experience that Ali, once set in motion, couldn't be stopped!

I was right. The doorbell rang at four o'clock on the dot. By then I'd been stressed and on alert for hours and was exhausted. I heard Mum open the door, then voices in the hallway, becoming gradually clearer.

'You go on up; you know the way.'

'Should do by now, shouldn't I?' Ali called as she mounted the stairs.

Her voice was louder than anything that had been heard in this house for a long while. My heart beat a little faster. It felt so weird. Ali was part of a different life, the world I'd been dreaming of for the past year but now here she was, opening the door into my sick room.

She had a rucksack slung casually over her shoulder and was carrying one of those chunky ring binders. Her hair had been straightened and it hung in a smooth, glossy curtain down her back. She wore a fitted sweater and tight jeans. She looked amazing, like a flawless high school actress in one of those American series. I felt a wave of pain rush over me. She was everything I wanted to be, everything I'd lost.

'Er . . . hi,' she said awkwardly.

I smiled painfully. Ali was my best mate; I didn't want to feel like this: bitter and jealous.

But I did.

I looked across at her. She was still hovering nervously in the doorway, clutching her large blue folder tightly to her chest and biting her bottom lip. And just for an instant, I saw her again as she'd been the day she'd first arrived at our junior school. She'd stood nervously in front of the class as the teacher introduced her. She'd looked every bit the new girl, shy and unsure of herself. Then one of the boys in the back row had sniggered and a sudden look of defiance had flickered across her face. That stubborn confidence had kicked in. She'd glared across the classroom at him and his mouth had clamped shut immediately. In that instant she'd become the Ali I knew: strong and fearless but now, eight years later, she stood in nearly the same position, looking slightly down and to the right with her arms folded protectively about her. This time, though, it wasn't a new school she was scared of: it was me, her best mate. I felt the bitter pain of it in the pit of my stomach. It couldn't be happening like this. I had to do something!

I strained to find the old Sarah and put her warmth and enthusiasm into my voice. 'Look, don't just stand there. Come in. Sit down.'

The unfamiliar words sounded unnatural and stilted to my ear but something about them must have been right because they seemed to do the trick.

'Thought you'd never ask,' Ali grinned, dumping her bag and folder onto the floor. She swivelled the desk chair round and straddled it backwards, resting her arms against its high back.

'OK, so what did I do?' she asked.

I'd forgotten how direct Ali could be and she knew, she obviously knew everything I was thinking and feeling. I tried to catch my breath as panic wailed through me.

'I don't know. I—'

'Well, I make it a full year of the silent treatment. I sure must have done something to annoy you!'

I smiled weakly from my mountain of pillows. It wasn't exactly the most amusing thing she'd ever said but I could see she was making an effort so I strained to enter into the spirit of things. 'Yeah, well, I had to do something to get rid of you. You do tend to get on people's nerves, you know, Ali.'

'You cow!'

'You can't call me that! I'm an invalid: you've got to be nice to me.'

'I can call you whatever I want. You're my best mate, aren't you? W-well, aren't you?'

I stared down at my hands. My fingers were turning blue: circulation on the blink, again. 'Yeah, well . . . you don't have to . . . I mean, if you still want—'

'Don't be so stupid. Of course, I still want to. What d'you think I'm going to do – start getting all pally with Chloë or Sophie? That girl's still obsessed with those damn magazines, you know? She had one last month on ME. Now she thinks she's a world expert. She keeps giving me all this advice and won't believe that you're too ill for me to even pass on her stupid ideas. She wants to know if you've tried cold baths and aromatherapy oils. Right, well, there you go. I've done my duty and told you now . . .'

I smiled vaguely. Ali was speaking so fast, it was making my head spin. Her voice was like the rat-a-tat-tat of machine gun fire: a continuous flow I strained to follow. It was the same with Jack sometimes. I could understand individual words but they were coming at me so thick and fast, I couldn't put them together to make proper sense.

'Anyway, it's so cool now you're getting better. D'you reckon you'll be up to starting college, soon? It's all right, you know, nothing like school. And there's loads of people re-doing their GCSEs and to be honest, some of them aren't the brightest, so you'll catch up in no time. You can get special dispensations, too, like extra time in exams. I was talking to this guy at college with ME – actually, he's totally gorgeous; I

143

might make a point of meeting up with him again, purely to find out stuff for you, of course!

'Anyway, he managed to keep going at school a bit, even when he was really ill. So he hasn't actually missed any full years but he was telling me about how he does his exams in a separate room, like, quieter, away from everyone and they even let him take a break every twenty minutes or so and give him extra time and stuff . . .' Ali petered out as she saw the look on my face.

'Right, well, I'm obviously a complete failure, then, aren't I?'

'What? No! Why?'

'Well, I didn't keep going at school when I was really ill, did I? Don't you think I wanted to? I did my best, Ali, but you were there, you saw how it was. I just couldn't, could I? And I don't particularly want to hear about this really amazing guy who's managed everything so much better than me . . . because . . . because . . . I'm not going to be starting college any time soon. Can't you see? I can barely sit up; it takes me ten minutes to get over a trip to the loo! I'm not exactly going to be up to studying Shakespeare in the next few weeks, am I?'

'I-I'm sorry. I didn't know. I got carried away. I just want you to be well, again.'

'And you think I don't?'

Ali stared down at the carpet, her eyes full of tears. I couldn't remember the last time I'd seen her cry. Suddenly, all the anger drained out of me. It wasn't Ali's fault after all. It was just that I spent so much of my time wondering how I might have avoided all this, if I should have done things differently: rested more or even pushed myself that bit harder. Hearing about someone who seemed to have cracked the illness, to have done so much better than me, didn't exactly cheer me up.

Sometimes, it seemed like the entire world: the postman, half Mum's friends, even the guy who came to read the gas meter, all knew someone who'd had this illness and somehow managed better than me: got better quicker or achieved really amazing things despite being ill. All summer, through the open windows, I'd heard them telling Mum about this person or that and how well they were doing. I knew they were only trying to help, give me hope, I guess, but mainly it just made me feel even more useless and alone.

Ali couldn't have known all that though. Besides, I looked at the timer. Only four minutes before I had to rest again and there was something I desperately needed to know.

'Look, I'm sorry. It's just I've been stuck here for over a year and I'm doing my best but I don't seem to be getting anywhere very fast.'

Ali raised her head, 'Yeah but you're better than you were and I've read all the books and they say sometimes people, like particularly our age, get better really quickly, so you never know . . .'

I forced a smile onto my face. I'd heard it all before and had given up believing in miracles. All the same, I didn't know Ali'd been reading books about my illness. I was actually really touched that she cared enough to wade through them. I mean, we're not exactly talking bedtime reading here.

I didn't have time to think about that now, though. I looked back at the clock: three minutes to go. There was nothing for it; I'd just have to plunge straight in. I could feel my heart beating high up in my throat; it took a huge effort to keep my voice casual.

'Anyway, do you see much of Dan round college?'

'Oh, him. Naw, not really. It's a big place and he's in a different year, does different subjects, you know.' She shifted slightly in her seat. 'You heard from him, lately, then?'

'Just a card last Christmas but I haven't been up to seeing anyone, have I?'

Ali scowled at the wall behind me.

'Look, I know you don't like him but—'

'It's not that,' she said not quite meeting my eye. 'It's just . . . look, I wasn't going to tell you, not straight away, anyway but I'm not going to lie to you either. It-it's just, Dan, right . . .' She took a deep breath. 'He's going out with Chloë.'

Chloë! The hollow echo of her name bounced round my head. No! This couldn't be happening. It couldn't be true! Something was rising within me, reaching up from my stomach and spreading out across my chest. I knew when it reached my throat I'd start screaming. I had to do something to keep it down, at least while Ali was here. Desperately, I scanned my brain, searching for something to say, any funny little comment I could put between me and the pain.

'Oh well, they can take it in turns to use the loo in her en suite, can't they?' I finally managed.

'What?'

'Didn't she move to that house in the end? You know, the posh one with all those bathrooms.'

'Oh yeah. Yeah, she did. Sorry, I forgot she used to go on about that all the time.'

"Used to" – that just about summed it all up. My life was so far in the past that Ali couldn't even remember the things we used to joke about. And Dan . . . Dan was gone.

Ali looked concerned. 'Look, I'm sorry. Are you all right? I mean, really all right?'

I shrugged just as the alarm of Mum's cooking timer slashed through the air.

'I've got to rest now,' I said trying not to sound too relieved; I just wanted to be alone.

'Oh, right, yeah, sure. Look, can I come back again, tomorrow?'

'No. I get washed up – I mean, *out*.' I gestured randomly towards the radiator as though that might clarify matters. My brain was somewhere far away. 'I can't do stuff every day,' I finally managed to explain.

Ali frowned at the radiator, then turned back to me. She was looking really concerned now. 'R-right, well, a couple of days, then. Friday OK?'

'Yeah, fine,' I muttered, sliding down my pillows. I would have agreed to anything just to get her to go. I was desperate to be alone, to escape back into that other world where none of this had happened.

'You look after yourself,' she ordered as she collected her stuff and, in a moment, she'd disappeared out the door.

I stared at the spot where she'd last stood and felt the emptiness grow around me. Mum came in to check I was OK. I pulled the covers over my head and muttered something about needing to rest and she left again.

I closed my eyes and tried to slip back into the world of memory and fantasy that had sheltered me for so long but it was no good. I couldn't summon up the images I wanted. I no longer saw myself happily entwined with Dan, just vision after vision of him and Chloë together. Every time I closed my eyes I saw her with her dark hair and perfect pale skin and those huge brown eyes.

Dan and Chloë

I couldn't bear the thought of it. And it wasn't just those two. It seemed that everybody was moving on without me: Ali starting college, Jack doing his GCSEs and Dan . . .

Dan and Chloë

If my life had stopped, I wanted the world to stand still and wait for me, not for everyone to go on doing the stuff I dreamt of every day.

Dan and Chloë. No, it couldn't be true!

And why me? What had I done that this terrible thing had happened to me? Why not to Chloë with her backbiting and meanness or to Sophie with those ridiculous magazines or to Dan? Let him see how it felt to get dumped by the entire world. Why not to Johnny or Steve with their stupid pranks or even to Jack or Ali? I screwed my eyes up tight. Anyone, I thought, *anyone,* just not me. I felt guilt rise, like bile, in my throat. Ali was my best mate, Jack my brother.

Why was I such a horrible person to wish this on them when all they'd ever done was try and help me?

Dan and Chloë

Image after image circled my brain: Dan and Chloë at the cinema, in the playground where we'd kissed, walking down a college corridor holding hands before striding out into the sunshine. It was all too much.

I could barely eat my dinner. Mum looked worried but I told her I was just tired after seeing Ali. I sent her away again saying I needed to rest. I couldn't bear to have her in the room; I couldn't bear to be alone.

Dan and Chloë

I wanted to get rid of the images but they formed an endless loop in my brain. I longed to escape, to leave them behind with my aching body, to sleep, if only for a few minutes. Some hope! I spent the night writhing round my bed, thoughts of Dan and Chloë blocking my sleep at every turn.

By morning I was faint with exhaustion, my body etched with pain. It carved its way into every muscle, sliced across my head and burned through my throat. I couldn't sit up or talk or bear any light. I turned my face from the food Mum brought, swallowing only a few mouthfuls. I was as ill as I'd ever been. The only difference now was that I no longer cared. I stared, zombie-like, up at the ceiling or across at the insistently cheerful yellow of my bedroom wall. I saw only my own pain reflected back at me and the thought of Dan and Chloë which seemed to be eating me up from the inside out.

By early afternoon I was overcome by sheer exhaustion. My eyes darted about behind their closed lids, following the images that raced feverishly through my sodden brain. They began to dissolve into each other, each one slipping a little further from reality. Chloë knelt in a child's sandpit, marking out an X with the sharp edge of her spade. She smiled up at Dan on the highest rung of the climbing frame. He leant over too far and then he was falling, falling, the scarred nape of his neck exposed and at last, I was slipping into sleep.

I started awake as the metallic buzz of the doorbell slashed through the house. My whole body was on alert. What was so important that it had ripped my sleep from me, robbed me of my one pitiful escape? I strained to listen as Mum opened the front door.

'He-*llo*,' the cheerful voices pitched upwards. 'Sorry to bother you but we were just wondering how you felt about God.'

I smashed my fists against the mattress and let out a blood-piercing scream. I didn't notice the slam of the front door, Mum's dash upstairs or the alarmed retreat of the Jehovah's Witnesses. The scream inside my head was so loud that it drowned everything else out. I felt it escape through my mouth, my fists, my legs. All the usual pain was submerged in a sea of fury as anger and adrenaline gave me more energy than I'd had for the past year. All the sadness, all the grief, all the rage that had built up during that time seemed to explode out of me.

'It's not fair!' I screamed.

Mum dashed into the room. 'Sarah! Please! Stop it!'

But I wouldn't, couldn't stop, not for her or anyone. I slammed about the bed, crying out that I'd never get better, never get well. *It wasn't fair!*

I thought I might go on like that forever, spend the rest of my life thrashing and screaming at the sheer injustice of it but then something weird happened. All the anger drained out of me and an overwhelming sense of weariness took its place. All of a sudden, I lay quite still; I felt nothing. It was like something inside me had quite simply switched off and I was floating above myself. I could see my body lying on the bed. I was aware of the pain gathering in my limbs, worse now after all that thrashing about but I couldn't actually feel anything. It was like it was happening to someone else.

I became aware of the drone of Mum's voice, pleading, coaxing, trying to reach me but it didn't stir anything in me. It was so far away, so unimportant. It meant nothing to me.

My breathing slowed and I felt more relaxed than I'd ever done before in my life. A wave of peace and safety flowed through me. I wanted to stay like that forever, cocooned from the world. Pain and loss were far away now, along with the agonising wrench of disappointed hope. I never wanted to feel another emotion again.

Somewhere, far away, Mum began weeping silently into her hands. I felt little hooks dig into my flesh, trying to drag me back, away from my place of safety. I ignored them. At some point, unnoticed by me, Mum slipped from the room, leaving me alone to drift peacefully on my sea of perfect calm.

151

I don't know how long I stayed like that, a few minutes or a few hours. I guess I needed the space, the escape. I just couldn't take any more: I'd reached my limit, more than passed it and needed a break before I was ready to get back to reality.

Part of me wanted to stay like that forever and there were certainly tough times over the next few years when I wished I had. But the fact was, I did return. Slowly, gently, I became part of the world again. I started to notice little things about me: birds singing, the smell of frying bacon, the sketch book lying on my bedside table. To begin with, I resisted. I didn't want to lose the easy, peaceful detachment I'd found that afternoon but gradually, I crumbled. I wondered how it might be to feel the sun on my skin again, to eat that delicious bacon, to draw new designs in my sketch book.

I looked at the world around me and thought that maybe, just maybe, I could face it again. I wasn't entirely sure. I really didn't know if I was strong enough to go on dealing with the illness, every minute of every day, to live without hiding behind fantasy but I wanted to give it a go.

I picked up my sketch book and flicked through it. The most recent drawings were weak, sort of shaky and rough but maybe, if I paced myself, I could improve. Perhaps, one day, I might even draw something worthwhile.

The door opened a crack. Mum edged her way in backwards, carrying a tray of my favourite meal: bacon and eggs. She looked at me nervously.

'I thought you might be hungry.'

I propped myself up on the pillows and nodded sheepishly. I could feel my mouth water as I looked at the golden eggs and sizzling strips of bacon.

'Yeah, I reckon I am.'

Chapter Thirteen

If I was going to start facing reality, then the first thing I had to do was get to grips with pacing and this time, I didn't mean just timing the odd activity but following a fully regimented schedule.

'I think you've got to decide what's important to you,' Mum said, 'what you really want to do. Then we can focus on those bits and not worry too much about the rest.'

But what did I want? I closed my eyes. I wanted Dan, his warm hands on my body, his lips brushing against my skin, his eyes staring intently down at me but that was the past. I wanted to go to college with Ali, have a laugh with my mates, go out to pubs and clubs like they were starting to but that was far in the future. I sighed and told myself, yet again, that I had to live in the present, the real world. It wasn't easy, though. Facing reality was like shining a bright light onto my miserable existence. I wanted to flinch from it but I made myself look. I saw my body throbbing in a darkened room, my mind trapped with nothing to look forward to but five minutes with Jack each day. Was there anything that could make my life more bearable? I took a deep breath and opened my eyes.

'I want to be able to speak to Ali on the phone, watch TV sometimes, draw again, have a wash every day . . . and sit up, like in a chair . . .'

'Right,' Mum said in a matter of fact tone. She was sitting business-like at my desk, pen poised over a fresh sheet of paper, ready to draw up plans. 'According to Joan, the secret is to break the activities down into tiny chunks, at least to begin with and have a rest after each one. So, if you just start with thirty seconds TV, then have a rest. Same for sitting up and drawing, I guess,' she paused for a moment and turned slightly so she could study my face carefully. She was clearly trying to work out how I was taking it all. I could see the calculation flitting across her eyes.

I nodded grimly from my pile of pillows; she went on, 'Phoning's going to be more difficult. Maybe, if you just try holding the phone up to your ear for the first week, get used to the weight of it again. And if that's too much someone online was talking about headsets. Perhaps we could get hold of one of those? We'll have to see how it goes. Then ring the home number for a while; make sure you can cope with the noise that makes before you even think about starting to talk. We'll draw up a timetable . . . but, Sarah, I think you really *have* to stick to it this time.'

'Yeah, all right, Mum. I know,' I grumbled, shifting irritably in bed. I had to do this, I knew I did but I didn't have to like it. 'Just one question, though. How do I have a thirty-second wash?'

'I've no idea,' Mum smiled ruefully, 'but I get the feeling we're about to find out.'

And so I began my new timetable. Mum's cooking timer became law. I threw all my energy into completing each day and then with infinite, soul-crushing slowness, building up the activities. It was hard, by far the hardest thing anyone had ever asked me to do. Far more difficult than following Dr Stoke's crazy plan of sending me straight back to school or going on that long journey to the Onslow Clinic because it depended on me being patient and single-minded, not just for a few hours but every second of every day.

Bad days were tough; I was in so much pain and felt like I was getting nowhere. It was good days that were the real challenge, though, the days my body lightened up enough for me to actually enjoy what I was doing. I desperately wanted to see more than the tiny snippet of a film I was allowed or to stay sitting up, looking out of the window. It took so much will power to switch the TV off and lie down again when the timer told me to.

It was worth it, though. Gradually, the peaks and troughs of my illness evened out and I started to feel better about things. Sure, I still had bad days and unexplained relapses but I was improving more steadily and with fewer false starts than I'd ever done before.

It was more than that, though. I actually started to look forward again. When I woke up in the morning,

156

it became easier not to drift back off into some fantasy world. Instead, I thought about what I was going to do that day and planned how I'd manage it. Sure, it wasn't fool proof and I often found myself dreaming of that other life, the life that might have been, but rarely with the same single-minded intensity as I'd done before. The world around me became gradually clearer; it seemed I'd found a way to move forward. Pacing was never going to give me my old life back but it could help me make the most of the one I actually had.

That Christmas, Mum, Dad and Jack clubbed together and bought me a laptop so I could get online from bed. It was second-hand and pretty beat up looking but things weren't great financially. Mum hadn't worked for eighteen months and after the mortgage was paid and the food bought there was, quite literally, nothing left. I couldn't help noticing that my laptop was a damn sight better than anything Jack got that Christmas.

'Are you sure he doesn't mind?' I asked Mum as she brought my Christmas lunch up.

'I doubt it. It was his idea, after all.'

'Really?'

'Don't look so surprised, love. It might not seem like it but he does occasionally think and he's actually got quite a good head on him, when he decides to use it.'

I bit my tongue. Christmas didn't seem the kindest time to disillusion her.

I ate my lunch and rested. Then I grabbed the laptop and got going. I had such a great time that afternoon: e-mailing Ali, looking at clothes shops and downloading loads of new music. It felt like the world was opening up to me again. I spent more than an hour online and the next four days flat out in bed with searing pains behind my eyes and image after image of the websites I'd visited flashing repeatedly through my brain; my arms hurt so much that I couldn't even hold a glass of water for two days!

I think that's what I hated most about the illness: you never got a day off, not even at Christmas. You forget that you simply can't take time out to celebrate or have an argument or explore a new computer and the next day your body reminds you. It sends out these sharp spirals of pain almost like it's punishing you for forgetting.

And always, at the back of your mind, that constant worry – what if? What if your body packs up again tomorrow and decides to snatch it all away from you? And I knew it could happen at any moment, not just if I was overdoing it. I mean, I could pace to within an inch of my life, do everything possible to stabilise my condition but I knew, at the end of the day, if it wanted to, the illness could pull the ground from beneath my feet and send me spiralling downwards again, for no reason at all.

I was lucky, though. The ME was gradually receding. I was stronger than I had been and within a week I found myself back on my old timetable. By the second week of the New Year, I was painstakingly adding five minutes computer time into my daily schedule.

I was doing a lot more these days – five minutes on the phone, half an hour sitting up, fifteen minutes TV, ten minutes sketching and reading, quarter of an hour seeing Ali or Jack and all this on top of washing and getting dressed. As I had to have at least half an hour's rest after each activity, as well as fitting in eating and a night's sleep, my life often seemed busier and more complicated than it'd done before I was ill!

It was an overcast day in early February when I stumbled across my first ME website. My brain felt as dull as the weather and by the time I got online, I'd completely forgotten what I'd been going to do there. My mind was submerged in a flu-like haze and I found myself googling ME . . . ME . . . ME . . . over and over as though pouring it out into the computer might somehow release me. Absent-mindedly, I clicked on the links. Mum had been trying to get me to visit these sites for weeks now but I hadn't wanted to. The illness had swallowed up enough of my life. The last thing I wanted was to waste even more time finding out about it.

Now, though, I found odd words and phrases jumping out at me and it wasn't the boring biological details of neural pathways and nerve endings that I'd come to associate with the illness. Instead, I found chat rooms and facebook groups where people were just talking about how they were getting on that day or stuff that didn't even have anything to do with ME, like which films they were watching or just some funny video clip they wanted to share with everyone.

I was a bit nervous about joining in to start with. Everyone seemed to know each other and they were chatting away and joking like old friends. Plus, some of them were loads better than me. I didn't think they'd be interested in anything I had to say but encouraged by Mum and Ali, I took the plunge and it was like the doors just opened for me. Pretty soon I had dozens of new friends and found myself chatting away with them most days if only for five minutes at a time. For the first time in two years, I was part of a group again and the best thing was I didn't feel like I had to push myself or make myself ill to join in. I just sort of fitted as I was.

'So, have you spoken to Andy yet, today?' Ali asked. It was spring again and the light from my half open curtains illuminated the irritating smirk across her face.

Andy was this guy I'd met on one of the forums. He was two years older than me but we'd become ill around the same age so we'd missed all the same sort of stuff. Plus, he was into art too. He drew cartoons. They were really clever and funny and sometimes they'd get published in the ME magazines. And, yes, OK, I was starting to wonder if there might be something there between us, other than the damn illness.

'Actually, he sent that picture through so we finally get to see what he looks like. Just give me a sec and I'll show you.'

I picked the laptop up from my bedside table and switched it on. It was getting easier to manage its weight these days. It booted up quickly too. I clicked Andy's picture open and waited for his face to pop up.

'There you go,' I said, twisting the screen round so Ali could see.

'Whoa! He's not exactly ugly, is he?'

'He's all right,' I muttered non-committally.

'Oh, come on, he's gorgeous. What's the matter? Is it because he's not got that soppy boy band look like D—'

'No, it's not that,' I said cutting her off. Since that first meeting, we hadn't actually talked about Dan. Ali'd skirted around the subject a few times but I always tensed up and changed it as quickly as I could. It wasn't that I was still living in some fantasy world where I thought we'd get back together. Our relationship was over; I'd accepted that but at the same time, I didn't want to hear about him and Chloë, together, living the life that'd been snatched from me.

'It's just, he probably doesn't even like me, you know,' I said nodding towards the photo of Andy.

'Yeah,' Ali mused, 'what with you being such a minger and all that.'

'Shut up,' I laughed and threw a pillow at her; it missed feebly just as Mum's cooking timer went off.

'Oh well, I'd better go, anyway. I've got to go round to Jess's and sort out my UCAS form.'

'Your what?' I didn't have the faintest idea what an UCAS form was or who Jess was for that matter. It was like that between me and Ali these days. She was still my best mate. I saw her three of four times a week now and the awkwardness of that first meeting had more or less evaporated but the shadow of our separate lives still hung between us.

Sometimes it seemed like we were talking different languages. We'd be chatting away, just like old times, and then one of us would say something, usually to do with Ali's college work or my ME and suddenly we'd look over and see the other one was completely lost. Then we'd have to enter into these laborious translations that, however hard we tried, never really got the full meaning across. We worked at our friendship and bridged the gaps but the gaps were there, none the less.

'Oh it's just some form for applying for uni,' Ali explained.

'Ah, right OK then. Have fun.'

I kept the smile fixed on my face until she'd left the room. I didn't want to think about what it'd be like when Ali went off to uni and left me behind altogether.

Instead, my mind turned to Andy. I swivelled the laptop back round so I could see his face staring back at me: sharp blue eyes, pale skin and black hair. Ali was right: he *was* good looking and despite what I'd said, I was fairly sure he did like me. I mean, he said I had a cute smile and that's not the sort of thing you say unless you fancy someone, is it?

The best thing about Andy, though, was the way he made me see that not everything had to be a loss. Don't get me wrong, the illness had stripped my life away and I'd still do anything for it not to be happening to me. Not going down a straight path, though, getting totally knocked off course, being different, I guess, sometimes made you see things from a more interesting angle, like the way Andy looked at the world and could instantly pick out the funny, ridiculous bits and put them into his cartoons.

I could feel myself changing too and not just the way people do after something major's happened to them. Sure, that was part of it but it was more than that, something to do with all those screwed up chemicals racing round my brain, all that muzziness and confusion. It seemed that the very way my mind worked, the pattern of my thoughts and feelings, was changing. I felt it in my vivid, fluey dreams with their flashing colours and feverish nightmares. It started to come out in my sketches, too. They were more fluid and abstract now, less about trying to copy the world and more about how I actually saw it. Ms Thompson would have been proud of me; it seemed I no longer thought in straight lines.

I'd been scratching out ideas for paintings in my sketch pad for some time but I was nervous of trying anything big, wondering how my body would cope with the mental and physical effort. All the same, I asked Mum to get me canvas and paint for my seventeenth birthday and that summer I finally felt strong enough to begin.

I managed two pictures that year, sort of companion pieces. In the first one, a grey figure, a young girl, stood in the foreground with her hands held up to either side of her head. She wore an indescribable expression of grief and pain. And the rest of her? Well, let's just say she was having a bad hair day!

I covered the background entirely in wax crayon, flooding the page with as many different colours as I could, all thrashing violently about in different directions. Next, I painted over the crayon with a thick layer of black so that, apart from the grey girl in the foreground, the canvas was a smooth layer of pitch darkness. Then I got the point of a compass and attacked the black background, scratching out thin lines so that the colours of the wax crayon beneath showed through like splinters of fireworks all clustering round the distraught solitary figure. She was besieged on all sides, her fragile frame attacked by swirling colours with the relentlessness of a nightmare. The picture was entirely devoid of rest or peace or even the tiniest scrap of stillness that might soothe the eye. I called it *Despair*.

'Death by wax crayon!' Ali exclaimed, cocking her head to one side and squinting into the canvas like she'd be able to see it better that way. 'It's really good, though. Like something proper you'd see in a gallery, you know.'

I didn't hold my breath. Ali's art appreciation skills were second only to a blind nun. Still, it was better than the reaction I'd got from Jack. He'd walked in one day just after I'd done the black background, before I'd scratched through to colours underneath. He'd stopped short, frowned at the picture for about two seconds, then turned to me and asked, 'What's all this black about, then? You turning into a Goth or something?'

The second picture was called *Hope* although strangely enough it had far more black in it than *Despair*. I guess that's the thing about hope, though – if everything's all bright and shiny, you don't need it, do you? Anyway, I covered this second canvas almost entirely in thick deepest black, leaving only a small irregular shaped patch of intense light in the top right-hand corner – a luminous mixture of yellows and white. It was pretty small but just big enough to see without straining. I didn't bother asking Jack's opinion!

I was actually quite pleased with the result. I even sent the pictures off to some art competition and I won a prize. All right, it was only a £30 voucher and I didn't come anywhere near winning or anything. I mean, we're not talking about a flourishing of talent to make three years of hell worthwhile or any of that rubbish but still, you know, it was something. Finally, a small good thing I could build on in this new life of mine.

Chapter Fourteen

I held my locker key up to the window and watched the sunlight glisten off its shiny metal surface. Then, taking the scissors from my desk, I snipped it free of the plaited cord I'd once used to hang it round my neck. I looked at it for a second longer before handing it over to Jack who sat perched on my bed, watching me quizzically.

'You want me to give it back to school?' he asked, looking mildly puzzled.

Quick on the uptake, my brother!

'You know there's not much point, don't you? I mean, the school's got loads of copies. Must have because someone else has been using your locker for ages now.'

I sighed. So much for my grand gesture! I sat down again in the armchair by the window. It'd been a good idea of Mum's to move it up from the living room. I was sick of my bed and it was nice to have a comfy seat now I was well enough to sit up a bit.

'And those, too,' I continued undeterred, nodding towards the pile of textbooks on my desk.

'But won't you be wanting those? I thought you were going to do your GCSEs at college when you were better.'

'Yeah, well, maybe but even if I do they follow different courses there, use different books. Ali said. Anyway, half of them are geography and there's no way I'm ever taking that again!' I shuddered at the all too vivid memory of trying to stop my head sinking onto the desk as Mrs Wallace ran through her never-ending list of Brazilian exports.

'Wallace'll be most upset,' Jack grinned.

'Yeah, I'm sure she'll be losing sleep over it.'

He got up and started flicking through the books. 'Hey, can I have this history one? It's just I've lost mine and they make you pay five quid if you don't hand one back at the end of the year.'

'Whatever, Jack. Just make sure they all go back, OK? I don't want to find them under your bed in ten years' time.'

'Yeah, all right,' he muttered mutinously. He dropped the key into his pocket and scooped the books up under his arm. If any of them found their way back to school, it'd be a miracle. Still, I'd done my bit. Me and school were officially finished.

'You'd better go now, anyway; I've got to rest; I'm going shopping with Ali soon.'

'Hey, you getting my birthday present?'

'It's meant to be a surprise.'

Jack snorted. 'Yeah, right! Like I haven't told you a million times. I was just gonna say, make sure you get

Part Three and not Part Two, OK?'

'Look, if you don't leave me in peace, my brain'll be that muzzed up I'll probably end up buying you a Barbie!'

'Yeah, well, as long as it's the one with white frills and pink hearts on her dress.'

He left the room, smirking at his unbelievable wit.

I got up and drew the curtains shut. The light was pouring in now. I couldn't believe another year had passed and it was spring again, nearly Jack's birthday. He'd be sixteen this year and leaving school in the summer. I'd be eighteen, myself, in a few months.

I flopped down on the bed and stared up at the over-viewed patch of ceiling above me. I didn't mind people moving on so much these days. I mean, I still did a bit. There was part of me that ached to be going on those long train journeys with Ali to visit far-flung universities but I was more chilled out than I used to be, probably because I had more of a life myself. I was working steadily on my art and making more friends online. In fact, I'd even taken on a semi-official role as "welcomer" on one of the sites, helping reach out to new people. It felt good to be useful, finally the relief of helping others rather than everything being centred around me and my needs all the time. Plus, I could remember all too well how scary and lonely those first few months were. Just wish I'd known other people out there going through the same stuff sooner. I guess I had to be ready to accept the illness enough to look for them, though.

Then there was Andy. I closed my eyes and his image flickered beneath my lids. I smiled to myself.

He'd started uni last year. Well, that is he was doing a course with the Open University. He wanted to get a law degree and become a human rights lawyer which, I had to admit, was a tad more dynamic than any ambition Dan'd ever had. He'd even introduced me to the OU, made me look at all their stuff online.

I sighed. I couldn't think about that now. Ali'd be here soon and I had to get some rest. I took a few deep breaths, feeling the air flow smoothly in and out of my lungs, making sure it reached right down to my stomach. It was a technique I'd learnt from all the relaxation exercises Mum had got me to try and it helped a bit, particularly at times like this when my body was putting itself on alert, ready to go out.

It was still a big thing, you see, going out. I'd only really done it a few times and this'd be the first time with Ali. I couldn't walk very far so I had to use the wheelchair. I didn't mind so much. I mean, of course, what I really wanted was to stroll down the street like everyone else. Actually even better than that would be to go out without having to carefully re-arrange my energy for the day and plan everything down to the zillionth detail so I didn't do too much and make myself worse. Still, it was so cool being able to see the world again, look up at the sky, choose stuff for myself in shops or just see faces other than those of my family! Using the wheelchair and having to plan a bit seemed a pretty small price to pay in exchange.

Downstairs, the doorbell rang. I got out of bed and tidied my hair in the mirror and then left my room, closing the door behind me. My balance was still a bit dodgy so I gripped the banister to steady myself as I dashed downstairs.

Mum was in the hallway, explaining the intricacies of the wheelchair to Ali.

I sat on the bottom step to put my trainers on.

'All right,' Ali nodded but Mum's concentration was firmly fixed on the chair.

'These are the breaks,' she explained, pointing towards the rubber pads on the wheels. 'She works those herself but for heaven's sake, make sure you both agree on when you're stopping or she'll go flying! There is a seatbelt but she won't use it . . .'

I finished tying my laces and glared at Mum.

'Yes, he-llo! I am here, you know!'

She continued to ignore me.

'Don't worry, love,' she said to Ali. 'She's not had her phone call from Andy yet today and she's always in a foul mood till then!' She turned away from us to open the lounge door. 'Right, I'd better leave you both to it. Just you make sure you're back by midnight, though, or I'm sorry but I'm going to have to ground you!'

'Yeah, very funny,' I called after her. 'Honestly, Ali, I swear, she gets worse by the day. Anyway, how'd it go yesterday?'

Ali pulled a face. She'd been on another one of her uni visits.

'Not great,' she admitted. 'I told the interviewer exactly what I thought of Shakespeare. Just because I want to do English doesn't mean I have to like him, does it? I mean, there *are* about five hundred years worth of other writers to choose from but I don't

170

think the professor, or whatever he was, saw it like that. I liked *the place*, though. You would, too. Maybe, if you keep getting better and stuff, you could come and do your A Levels there. We could share a flat or something.'

'Yeah, maybe,' I mused but I wasn't sure it was what I wanted. It was nice of Ali to offer and if I got well, I'd come and visit her loads but I didn't want to be her sad little sick friend tagging on to her ready-made life. Anyway, I wasn't even sure I wanted to do A Levels. It's weird, you know. I mean, if I hadn't got ill, I reckon I'd just have followed this totally straight path: taken my GCSEs, done my AS and A Levels and then gone to university to do maths, not because I particularly liked it but because I was good at it and everyone expected me to. But, strangely enough, now that route was closed to me, at least for the moment, it felt like the world was suddenly bigger, not smaller. It was like there were all these choices out there that I never would have considered before. I mean, I probably would take a few GCSEs, do the basics, you know, but then again maybe not. No-one but Andy knew yet but I was actually on the verge of signing up for the Open University, only a really basic beginners' course in arts, like about a zillionth of a degree, but who knew where it'd lead. At this rate, I might even be starting uni before Ali!

'Earth to Sarah!' Ali's voice startled me. 'Three guesses as to who you're thinking about. So have you sorted anything out about him coming to visit, yet?'

'What Andy?'

Ali gave me her best Homer Simpson D'oh look.

'Depends if Mum and Dad let Jack go away for this week at Easter.'

Jack's mate had invited him to Spain with him and his family. Mum and Dad didn't really want him to go, of course. They thought he should be revising for his GCSEs but who knew, they might just cave in.

'You see, Andy really needs a room to himself so he can lie down when he has to rest. I mean, Jack could sleep on the sofa but then he'd be wandering in and out of his room all the time to get stuff. He really needs to go away.'

'Your Mum and Dad'll probably let him go though, won't they? I mean, he'd still have the other week of Easter to revise and let's face it, he's not going to do it, is he?'

'You know that and I know that but Mum still has this deluded idea that he's going to work and actually get some GCSEs . . .' I glanced at the clock on the hall table. 'We'd better get going,' I said moving over to the chair. 'Look, you know once we're outside, I can't talk much what with all the noise and stuff going on.'

'Sure, no problem,' she assured me but knowing Ali, I didn't hold out much hope. As it happened, we hadn't even reached the end of the drive before she started up. She'd just manoeuvred me awkwardly out of the front door and nearly propelled me into a rose bush when she announced, to the world in general, 'It's a shame we're not gay!'

'What?' I raised my eyes to heaven. All the same, I couldn't help smiling. You see, Mrs Wilson, our next-door neighbour – her of the circuit training and seaweed baths – had been making a beeline for us but on hearing Ali's statement, she'd darted back behind her hedge in alarm.

As usual, Ali was oblivious to all this. Or was she? I often wondered.

'Well,' she continued, nodding cheerfully to a startled Mrs Wilson, 'you're disabled, I'm black and we're both women. If only we were gay as well, we'd have it *all* between us, you know, all the major discrimination groups.'

'Yeah, right, whatever. Just shut up and push the chair, all right?'

'Yes, ma'am,' she replied and clamped her mouth tight shut as she climbed the hill. She panted slightly as we turned the corner into the row of shops. Give her her due, she did manage to keep quiet until we passed the chip shop but then I heard a sharp intake of breath behind me.

'Don't look now,' she hissed into my ear, 'but Chloë's in there.'

I turned and saw her, waiting in line. Her face was familiar but different somehow, all grown-up looking. I reminded myself that it'd been three years since I last saw her. She stood, leaning against the counter, gazing vacantly at her snow-white good looks in its reflective steel surface.

'Is she still going out with Dan?' I shrugged my shoulders slightly, trying to make the question sound casual.

'What? No way! That lasted for all of like three minutes. I mean, even Dan worked out she was a complete cow soon enough . . . W-why? You don't still like him, do you?'

'No, of course not!' I answered automatically. But then an image came into my mind and it wasn't Dan but Andy, Andy with his piercing blue eyes, his intelligence and his passion, and I realised, with a slight shock, that I really *didn't* care about Dan anymore.

'Right, we're here,' Ali announced as we reached the shop. She struggled to hold the door open and manoeuvre the cumbersome chair through it at the same time.

Luckily, someone darted forward to help us or I probably would have ended the day face down on the pavement. Ali and I nodded our thanks, then made our way to the games aisle.

A lad, about Jack's age, stood scanning the new releases. He looked alarmed when he saw us heading towards him and shifted awkwardly from foot to foot before shuffling off a few paces to make room for us.

'Right, what's this thing called?' Ali asked.

'I dunno. "Death Row Psycho Three" or something like that.' I searched in my bag for the scrap of paper Jack had given me. 'Apparently, the three's *very* important.'

Ali took the piece of paper, looked down at the title and then frowned up at the endless rows of games before us. She turned to the lad who'd now retreated several more paces.

'Oy,' she called.

He looked round nervously, clearly hoping she was talking to someone else. No such luck!

'Yeah, you, Mr Shiftyfoot, where do I find this?' She passed him the piece of paper, then added, 'The three's *very* important.'

'I-I don't work here,' he stuttered.

'Yeah, all right, I didn't ask for your life story. I just want to know where the game is, OK?'

He looked scared, an effect Ali often had but nodded silently and pointed towards the row of new releases.

'Thank you,' Ali smiled sweetly; his face froze in complete terror.

Mind you, I didn't look so hot myself. I'd just seen the price! I checked my money. I had enough, *just*. I hesitated then took a deep breath before announcing, 'All right, let's get it.' After all, Jack, for all his faults, had been a pretty good brother to me over the last few years.

The queue for the single working cash desk was a long one. The girl behind it looked stressed and flustered. I was tired and it seemed that we moved painfully slowly up the queue. Worse still, when we finally reached the front, I realised that the counter was so high, I'd have to stand up to reach it. I heaved myself out of the chair and handed the game over. It was at that point I became aware of the commotion behind me.

I turned to see Ali flailing her arms about wildly and wailing, 'It's a miracle! She can walk!' before sinking to her knees behind the chair.

A tidy-looking woman, half way down the queue, tutted loudly, 'Ought to be more responsible when she's in charge of a poor wee handicapped lassie like that!'

Ali bounced up and reeled round to face her, a maniacal smile spreading across her face. 'It's day release,' she announced with unnerving glee. 'They let me out once a week to push cripples but I'm asking for another one next time. This one's defective! Look, she's on her feet!'

A collective gasp rippled through the queue as Ali uttered the word cripple. I opened my mouth to tell her that, cripple or not, I'd personally kill her if she didn't shut up but I was distracted by the fraught cashier who was clearly trying to attract my attention. She was starting to look quite desperate.

'You know this is an 18 certificate, don't you? Have you got any ID?'

She seemed slightly embarrassed. I mean, she fairly obviously wasn't even eighteen herself. I felt a bit sorry for her, actually. Honestly, trust Jack not to mention the minor fact that technically, I couldn't even legally buy his birthday present!

'No, sorry, just cash, I'm afraid.' I opened my purse wide to show her. 'But I *am* eighteen.'

The lie slid easily from my lips. I'd had plenty of practice. After all, I used to do it nearly every week when Ali and I had claimed to be fifteen or eighteen or whatever it took to get us into the cinema to see the film we wanted. Then I realised with a shock that actually, I *was* nearly eighteen.

The girl hesitated, taking in my un-made-up face and my hair cut which hadn't changed since I was fourteen. Then she glanced at the lengthening queue which was starting to shuffle and mutter its discontent and at Ali who was brushing down her jeans, that mad smile still plastered across her face. She clearly decided that a tabloid set-up along the lines of "Shock!

Horror! Gory games sold to underage girls!" was unlikely to hire a wheelchair as a prop or, for that matter, a complete maniac to push it!

She smiled nervously and scanned the game through the checkout. I handed the money over quickly, before she could change her mind.

'OK,' Ali began as soon as we'd left the shop, 'maybe I did go a bit far but you've got to admit, they're never going to call you "a poor wee handicapped lassie" in *that* shop again!'

'Yeah, but Ali, that's mainly because they're never going to let me in there, again, isn't it?'

We were so wrapped up in our conversation that we completely failed to see the danger coming: Chloë, with her face stuck in a punnet of chips. The collision occurred before any of us noticed.

'Oh!' Chloë squealed, the pitch of her voice somewhere between embarrassment and alarm. None of us really wanted to see each other but it was too late now.

'Er, hi,' Chloë stammered looking from me to Ali in bewilderment.

I sighed.

'Look, just give us a chip, eh, Chloë.'

They smelt good. Their strong vinegary scent reminded me of fresh air and health. I stretched out to take one; Chloë's face tightened. She glanced nervously towards the wheelchair, like she wasn't quite sure if what I had was contagious.

Ali had been quiet for some time which was always a dangerous sign.

'You're not gay, are you, Chloë?' she suddenly blurted out.

Chloë reared back in alarm, nearly dropping the chips into my lap. She scanned the street nervously to see if anyone had heard.

'No, of course not!' She had a look of outraged horror on her face, like Ali had just accused her of murdering a litter of puppies.

'Oh well,' Ali shrugged, turning her head from side to side, deliberately mirroring Chloë's scrutiny of the street, 'in that case, I'm afraid we really can't be seen talking to you. We've got an image to protect here!'

And with that she pushed the wheelchair forward and back down the hill, leaving an outraged Chloë far behind.

'I'm never *ever* going out with you again!'

I was sitting on the bottom stair in our hallway, trying unsuccessfully to kick my trainer off between peals of laughter. Ali had collapsed into the wheelchair beside me shaking with uncontrollable giggles.

'Did you see the look on her face?' she asked, 'That has to be a Chloë classic!'

'Yeah, but I never did get my chip, did I?'

'That'll be our next trip out: *Operation Chip Shop.*'

'Just give me a few weeks, eh? It's going to take me that long to get over this one! You know, though,' I added as I watched Ali trying to perform some sort of wheelie in my chair, '*you're* the one who should be housebound and that's just for public safety.'

At that moment Mum emerged from the kitchen carrying a cup of tea.

'What on earth's going on, here?' she asked.

Ali and I exchanged glances then doubled up in a fresh burst of laughter.

'You kind of had to be there, Mum,' I finally managed to splutter out.

And, with a shock, I realised this was the first time in years Mum *hadn't* been there. For what seemed like an eternity, she'd been my constant companion: bringing my food, helping me wash, looking after me, sorting out my timetable, cheering me up, encouraging me to keep going. Now, at last, I was beginning to be able to do things on my own again or at least with Ali. I stopped short and spun round to face Mum. I could tell from the expression in her eyes that she was thinking exactly the same as me and as she turned away into the lounge, the smile that spread across her face was the widest I'd seen in years.

Author's Note

I've taken some liberties with the reality of ME services available in my portrayal of the Onslow Clinic. Sadly, this comprehensive service does not currently exist although something similar was once offered by the ME Centre in Essex. I have included it, both for the purposes of explaining this complex illness, and also because it's my fervent hope that one day such services will be available locally for all ME sufferers. In addition, home visits for the severely affected are essential. Currently, house and bed-bound sufferers, in great pain, often endure long journeys, just to get help and advice. As ME generally deteriorates with over-exertion, this is clearly counter-productive.

I hope this novel can do a small amount to raise awareness of a condition which is often dismissed as trivial but which, in reality, robs its sufferers of years, sometimes decades of their lives.

Acknowledgements

I'd like to thank everyone who's given their time and energy to help me with this novel. Special thanks go to my dear friend, Zoë Williams, Susie and Madeleine Green, Grainné O'Riordan, Lydia Bradburn and above all my mother, who has read and re-read this book at all stages of its creation and always been there with encouragement and advice.

I'd also like to mention Jill Moss, who allowed me to make reference to her excellent book *Somebody Help ME*. This has since been replaced by *A Ray of Hope*.

Useful Addresses

M.E. Association
7 Apollo Office Court
Radclive Road
Gawcott
Bucks
MK18 4DF
01280 818964
www.meassociation.org.uk

Action for M.E.
PO Box 2778
Bristol
BS1 9DJ
Tel: 0845 123 2380
or 0117 927 9551
www.actionforme.org.uk

For Children and Young People:

The Young ME Sufferers (Tymes) Trust
Holder of the Queen's Award for Voluntary Service:
the MBE for Volunteer Groups
Tymes Trust
PO Box 4347
Stock
Ingatestone, CM4 9TE
0845 003 9002
www.tymestrust.org

Association of Young People with M.E.
AYME
10 Vermont Place
Tongwell
Milton Keynes
MK15 8JA
08451 23 23 89
www.ayme.org.uk

For the Severely Affected:

The 25% group
21 Church Street
Troon
Ayrshire
KA10 6HT
01292 318611
www.25megroup.org

USA

The CFIDS Association of America
PO Box 220398
Charlotte, NC 28222-0398
704-365-2343
www.cfids.org

Australia

ME/CFS Australia Ltd
C/O ME/CFS Australia (Victoria)
PO Box 7100
Dandenong VIC 317
(03) 9793 4500
www.mecfs.org.au

Canada

National ME/FM Action Network
512, 33 Banner Road
Nepean
ON K2H 8V7
613-829-6667
www.mefmaction.net

FM-CFS Canada
99 Fifth Avenue
Suite 412
Ottawa ON
Canada K1S 5P5
1-877-437-HOPE (4673)
www.fm-cfs.ca